THE WEREWOLF ASYLUM
A Novelette

Gareth Barsby

ISBN 978-1-4467-7321-5

For Mum and Dad

'I became insane, with long intervals of horrible sanity.'
Edgar Allan Poe

Breathing heavily, Martin made his way off of the basement floor, and stumbled about, the chill of the room clearing his head. The night was over, and he had reclaimed his humanity at last. This precious, natural form though, he would lose it again in a matter of time, and it would be lost the night after that too. Thus, he would retreat to his basement every night in order to contain his moments. That cold, damp basement. That soothing basement. That peaceful basement. He never kept anything down there; it only seemed to exist to be empty. Fewer things meant more solitude though. Solitude was good. No-one judges you when you are alone. Nobody to bark at you or kill you or say anything less than complimentary. Every night, he would see those faces. Snarling, jeering faces without bodies.

Those faces weren't here though. Nobody in the soothing basement except him and a lone spider. What was there to do before the inevitable? Pray? Prayer used to be his answer to all, but it did little now. Did the Lord not care about his condition? Did he just not know? He was the Lord, he had to know. So maybe he didn't care after all.

What did he do before he preyed...prayed? He drank. Yes, that was what he did. Should he do that now? Would it calm him before he became that other him? Would it make his nightly self less dangerous? Back in the days when he would drown his sorrows, his friends would comment on how languid and vulnerable he was after excessive intoxication.

It was a foolish thing to think even to himself. This other him, this creature that came out, it couldn't be cured by something so crude, so simple. Controlling it was out of the question. He had this very same train of thought yesterday, and the day before that, and every day since he had this condition. These thoughts even occurred when he was trapped in that other form, even if his body did not respond to his mind.

So what was there to do? Not think, perhaps. Thinking brought more bad than good most of the time anyway. He was probably not put on this earth to think anyway. There were people out there that did it better than him.

What was there to do? Nothing. His recent mania had lost him his job, so there was no work to be done, and nothing was all that really could be done. He was not one to do something, so he decided to do nothing. Perhaps the more he did nothing, the more his nightly self would do nothing as well. Climbing up his basement's wooden stairs, the creaking making him shudder slightly, he aimed for his favourite chair. With his lack of income, he may have to say farewell to it soon, so it would be best to savour every moment with it. Yes, he would spend the whole day there, until night falls and he did what had to be done.

Same thoughts every day.

He had spent an hour or so doing what he had planned to do, when suddenly there came a knock at the door, which pounded in his head like a migraine. Someone knew what he had done, knew who he was. The police. They knew what he had once done at night and had come to arrest him.

Another knock came.

Martin told himself he would do nothing, and if he did answer that door, he would be breaking his own promise.

Another knock. A voice.

'Excuse me. May I speak to you?'

It did not sound like the police. Still, Martin remained in his chair. That man at the door did not know about his condition and when he was around people who didn't know, he would be distracted by what they would do if they did know. Do nothing, do nothing. That's what you were supposed to do today.

'Please answer this door. I wish to talk.'

If he was going to disappoint this man, it would just give him more guilt and he certainly did not need more of that. Scrambling from his chair in a disjointed dance, he made his way towards the door. His gut felt like it was being clenched as he approached the door, with the inward suspicion it could still be the law.

There at the door stood a thin man, with a serious look on his face that sent Martin stumbling backwards. As he lifted himself up, Martin noticed how much the man resembled an undertaker, his regal top hat and coat highlighting the shoddy appearance of Martin's abode.

'Thank you for letting me in,' said the man. The tone was friendly, yet he did not smile. 'My name is Dr. Harlston. I am pleased to make your acquaintance.'

Harlston held out his hand for Martin to shake, but Martin stood still, his lip quivering.

Putting down his hat on the table, making it look more presentable in the process, Harlston smiled slightly. He slowly entered the house, keeping his coat on due to the chill. 'I know you are anxious. Your kind usually is.'

He knew.

Letting loose a frantic scream, Martin scurried away, knocking over furniture as he did so. As excited as he was, all it took was Harlston saying, 'Do not be like that', and Martin ended his frenzy.

'You know about...'

Harlston nodded. 'It is my duty to know about it. Shall we talk about it over a cup of tea?'

'I'm...I'm...'

Harlston raised an eyebrow. 'Yes?'

'I'm sorry. I don't have any tea. I have little money.'

Harlston's smile grew wider. *'Don't worry. At least you are honest. I like that.'*

'What are...are you here about?'

'You are troubled about your condition, are you not?' The smile disappeared.

No answer came from Martin.

'You feel uncomfortable living here, among those...how shall I say, unassuming.'

Clenching his fists, Martin brought himself to speak. *'How do you know...'*

'I know about these things. I have been dealing with your kind for years. Besides, the holy noise coming your house...'

Harlston found himself interrupted by Martin's face right up close to his own. *'Can you help me?'*

'That is why I am here. I work at an institution meant for people with your infliction. There, we will help you repress those transformations you have, give you proper shelter to contain you when you're more...active, and you can meet others with your condition. I even think I may find a cure...'

It was the law.

'A madhouse?'

'I wouldn't say that. Going there is entirely your choice though, and will cost you a little. If you want to remain disturbing the neighbours and waking babies, I will not stop you.'

Martin said nothing, and returned to his chair. After he did so, Harlston approached him, making him squirm in his seat.

'At least you are wise enough to contain yourself. Have you not read the news?'

Martin sat upright. *'What's in them?'*

'I am pretty sure you can guess on your own.'

Hearing this, Martin shrunk back. He knew what he did at night, and could not remember escaping from his basement, but couldn't help but ponder some possibilities.

'I suppose you may want some time alone so you can consider my proposal...'

'No!' Martin sprung up, grabbing Harlston by the collar. 'I want to go.'

'Are you sure?' Harlston sniggered. 'Oh, what am I saying? Of course you are.'

'Yes!'

Still holding tight onto Harlston, Martin let the doctor inject him and toss him into a carriage, taking him to where his thoughts had lead him. Maybe the Lord did care.

2nd January 1887

Today I received a new patient, courtesy of my associate Dr Harlston. I suppose there is no better way for our institution to begin the New Year. It may also be just as well, given the death of Mr. Stantford last week.

His name is Martin Clentsworth. He claims he gained his condition last month, but how he acquired it is a blur to him. When I asked him if anybody else knew about what he had become, he told me he preferred not to say. This, slightly to my discomfort, did not bother me. Still, I hope I will make him comfortable enough that he will be willing to tell me anything.

'Have you tried repressing your transformations at all?' I asked him as I escorted him to Stantford's old cell.

'No...no, I haven't.'

'They never have, have they?' said Harlston as he walked besides me, 'That was why he was ecstatic to hear about our services.'

We placed him in the cell, and I asked him if there was anything he needed. 'No,' he said, 'Just leave me alone, please.' Feeling it was best to honour his request, I closed the door behind him.

'Are you sure you should have given him Stantford's cell?' asked Harlston, plucking his moustache.

'We are low on rooms at the moment,' I replied, 'and I certainly do not want any of the patients having to share. I am also pretty certain that there is no "curse" associated with that cell, nor am I dishonouring the man's memory.'

'I still find his death ironic,' Harlston chuckled to himself. 'All those long days worried that his friends were going to turn against him and murder him, and he dies of an aneurysm.'

'It is a shame that he died before he could properly repress his transformations.'

'Indeed. And it is a shame that there are still werewolves out and about, if the media is anything to go by.'

Ah yes. Even after we receive new patients, and those patients occasionally leave us, I still hear of attacks from some wild creature around this area.

'Do you think it could be...it?' asked Harlston.

'Possibly,' was my response, 'but you should know that we should never get our hopes up.'

'Of course.'

Having experiments to return to, Harlston departed, leaving me to my patients. The halls were unusually quiet today, and while that may be in some ways more unnerving to me than the usual cacophony of wails and anguish, at least it means conversation would be easier.

I found myself tempted to go back to Clentsworth's cell, just to see if I can make him remember how he gained his condition. He apparently received it during Christmas time, a significant period for lycanthropy. Still, he wished to be left alone, so I should leave him alone until he calls for me.

Should I speak to Enfeld then, I thought. I doubt he wants me to speak to him. Smertall? He is doing rather well, and making him remember his past may disrupt his recovery.

I instead chose to speak with Mr. Gramson, who I found sitting in his cell as if silently contemplating something. He was in a thoughtful mood, so there were likely thoughts he wanted to share with me.

Gramson let me enter his room, and I must say, he was certainly calmer than he usually was. When he was first admitted here, I remember him clawing at the walls as if to uncover a secret doorway, screeching at what was outside the window and always succumbing to his nocturnal metamorphosis. He rarely ever wanted to speak, and his willingness to do so has given me a moment of hope.

'Hello,' he said, waving slightly.

'I just wanted to ask you about how well you are dealing with your condition.'

He spent another minute in quiet thought. 'I believe I am doing quite well.'

'Are you sure? I still see you succumbing at night...'

'I think tonight I will be able to repress.'

'Are you sure?'

'Yes. I've...forgiven myself.'

That tiny spark of hope grew. 'Have you really forgiven yourself?'

'I believe I have...'

'If you have, I congratulate you.' I placed a hand on his shoulder, and brought him closer. 'Most werewolves go through life eternally regretful.'

He released himself from my clasp, and moved away. 'I know.'

We had further discussion after that, but it was the same subjects he always spoke about to me. His wife's reaction to his lycanthropy, how he dealt with it, how he feels about being here. He is repetitive, but the more we talk about his problems, the more he will deal with them. Also, he usually has something complimentary to say about me.

After I leave his cell, making sure I open and shut the door as quickly as possible, the quiet that the asylum once had was replaced by the usual cluttering and noise. It was not because the patients had begun their transformations, but rather most of them were remembering their misdeeds and their troubles. It has all become a routine at this moment, yet I still wish to silence them. To eradicate their beasts.

That's what science is all about, trying to explain the unexplainable, and I've seen very few people try to explain lycanthropy. Those with it try to hide it, and I have seen no books written on the subject. So it seems Harlston and I are the only two left who will make the world comprehend this condition and uncover its secrets. In the many years we have tried though, we have actually found and uncovered little.

The news though. If *it* is out there, there may be hope.

And hope is what we need.

5th January 1887

Today has marked a significant discovery, but I must refrain from speaking of it right away, for there is less exciting news to note. We are not even a week into this year, and already our troubles have been increasing. This morning, Harlston made a visit to the moneylenders to see if we could get an extension on our loan, and it was rejected. I shouldn't be surprised; the nature of our operation means that we had to be as vague as possible, leading to less funding, but, despite the funding we do receive, as small as it is, and the income we get from some patients that pay us to be hidden away from the world, we are still lacking in the money department. Harlston has experiments planned and has lamented the lack of funding he needs to complete them.

That would be depressing enough to report, but there is something else I feel I must share before I speak of our discovery, perhaps to make that discovery seem more wondrous in comparison. Last night, Harold Smertall, for whom I had such hopes, went into a rage, creating such an unbearable cacophony and disturbance among the other patients. Those other patients had succumbed too, but until that night Harold was doing so well suppressing his nocturnal mayhem, that given a few more days, we would have discussed an early release. Enfeld may succumb every night, but that is to be expected given his personality. With Smertall, it seems an omen. If someone who normally exercises such willpower can succumb like this, what can be said about the others?

The only thing that can be done about this is to find an actual physical cure. Our lack of money at the moment may render that difficult, but thanks to Harlston, we have found something that could be a great aid to our research.

I have spoken at length before about the legendary 'permanent wolf'. A werewolf with a unique condition that means it stays permanently in wolf form, but unlike my patients during their transformations, it is an anthropomorphic, intelligent creature. I thought that, were I and Harlston to study it, we could understand this strange illness more and come closer to finding a physical cure for our patients' afflictions. While having heard plenty about it, I had doubted its existence, thinking that were it to exist, it would have come here, but now I know it – she – exists. And she is in our vicinity.

After Harlston had spoken to the moneylenders, he went out to search for information regarding our cause, and found some of it in a public house. As much as I disapprove of those places, I was willing to forgive it in this case. Harlston asked one man about rumours of a wolf-like creature, and that man said, 'Not a "wolf-like creature", just a wolf. It's just my mind has made it more than it actually was. I believe life is so mundane that sometimes, your memory tries to adjust itself to make your experiences seem more extraordinary than they actually are. A sort of mechanism for helping you get through things.

'What I'm trying to say is, I know I was mugged last night. It happens all the time in this city. I'm also certain that bugger was attacked by a wolf. It isn't really outside the realms of possibility. But my memory tells me the wolf spoke to me, in the beautiful voice of a woman.'

'What did she say?' Harlston had said.

'That I can't remember. I didn't focus on what she said, just that she said something.'

That episode Harlston described meant that the specimen was in this city, and, even if he wouldn't admit it, it seemed like the man believed what he saw.

After I met with Harold about his frightful behaviour last night – all he said about it was 'Memories can be such cruel things'

– we set out in the late afternoon to seek out the wolf, while trying not to make ourselves noticeable.

Harlston and I exited the asylum, rounding up our horses to pull the carriage we use to bring our patients to us. Not drawing attention to ourselves is quite difficult with that vehicle, with its strong resemblance to a hearse. After we trundled down the road that led to our asylum, we came to the city, with its rows of houses leaning to meet us. Being a rather harsh winter's day, with the soot-flecked snow still remaining on the cobbled pavements, the streets weren't that busy, to our fortune.

Looking at the homes, the public houses, the shops beginning to close down, it reminded me of where I grew up, where my family lived. Thus, I shut my eyes. One duty I find myself carrying out is making people forget their childhoods, so I have wondered if I should forget my own. My childhood is behind the creation of the werewolf asylum, so it cannot really be forgotten though.

Coughing from some smoke, Harlston put our carriage to a halt, and we both dismantled. My eyelids begged me for them to remain shut, but I needed to examine the city carefully for any sign of our subject. After I placed my feet on the ground, I turned my attention towards the snow. Walking down the streets with my head turned down, I looked for any unusual footprints. Pawprints.

'Are you sure searching that way is wise?' said Harlston, 'She could attack you from behind, you know.' I made myself upright, though I'm sure it was not because of his suggestion. 'And what,' Harlston continued, 'are we going to do if we find her? Will we actually ask her politely to join us?'

'She is supposed to be intelligent, and has the power of speech...'

'And she kills people. From what that man had said, she does not seem to be in a position to sit down with us with a plate of crumpets.'

'You did bring along your syringe with you, did you not?'

'Yes.'

'And I have a gun...' I looked around the streets. 'Though I hope I do not have to use it.'

'That's what I like about you,' said Harlston, 'Always optimistic in times like these.'

As we both trekked through the town, I looked around for any sign of our subject, made difficult by the distracting breeze. I began to wonder if she was still in this vicinity, or if she ran away somewhere. Or she could have even disappeared.

We continued walking through the buildings, but soon I didn't feel like I was even searching anymore, and was merely wondering about without any clear aim or goal. That man probably was just some drunken lunatic after all. Feeling my hope beginning to dwindle once again

'Hello there.'

That soft, feminine voice made both of us freeze in place before swiftly turning around. What was approaching us, however, was a woman, obviously of ill repute. I still stood frozen in place, knowing that she could affect this search. Thankfully, when she asked us what our business was, and we said nothing, she turned around and left in a huff. I daresay I do not wish to dwell on people like her.

Following that encounter, Harlston suggested we go separate ways to cover more ground. As I could sense dusk beginning to fall, so I agreed, knowing we would have to return to our institution soon.

As I was considering going back to my patients, as my search continued to be fruitless, Harlston came running back to me, almost skidding in the snow as he did so.

'Have you found something?'

Stumbling as he regained himself, Harlston replied, 'Not something. I think I have found her.'

I followed Harlston to where he thought he had seen our subject, hiding away in an alleyway, like a stray cat. When he brought me to the location, I saw a grey, furry lump hidden away in the darkness, resembling a stray dog more than a werewolf. I began to think this could be a joke until I got a closer look at her. Her 'bed' was a box, lined with urine and entrails, which made us both approach with caution. Nearing the creature, we saw an array of rats around her bed, huddling around as if she gave them warmth. When we arrived, they scurried away.

She awoke in an instant.

As she rose from her spot, I took this opportunity to observe her form more closely. She resembled a wolf, yet with elongated appendages and a curved body. 'Oh,' she said, and we were both frozen by English coming from the mouth of a creature like that. 'I have been waiting for this.' As she spoke, my eyes fixated on her jaws, long as a normal wolf's, yet covered with lips. The movement of her mouth hypnotized. Her voice sounded strangely mellifluous.

I stood in silence for a minute or so, and then I asked her, 'You have been waiting for us?'

'The Lord had told me that someday, people would come looking for me, and then I would be able to reveal myself to the world.'

'Lord?'

'You have not heard of him?' She grimaced at us, and I reached for the gun I kept in my coat pocket. 'He is going to create the world again, and he will do it through me. That is why I've been going about this city, eliminating those who displease the Lord.'

'Do you mean God?' Harlston asked.

'No, the Lord. He brought me here to give everyone my gift. This.' She then stood on her hind legs, which froze us once more, and stroked her fur, gesturing towards her form. Such an attitude towards her affliction gave me the appropriate energy to deal with this situation.

'I have come for you,' I said, 'because I have an institution which deals with people with a similar condition to you.'

She paused, and then she smiled, another thing rendered odd by her form. 'Take me there. I would like to meet those people.'

'Very well,' I told her. Harlston pulled out a syringe from his jacket pocket, and as she saw the implement, she backed away growling. Even her snarling grimace looked unreal. 'We don't intend to harm you; this is merely to calm you on the way.'

Her snarling immediately ceased. 'I can be calm on my own,' she told us, lying down to punctuate that point. We lifted her into the back of our carriage, and rode back, and she was oddly silent during most of the journey. However, when we neared the asylum, we noticed that dusk was falling, and I could already hear the patrons begin their transformation. While I was undoubtedly guilty for not being there to help them suppress their canine forms, some small part of me thought this was fortuitous, just so we could see her reaction to her brethren.

As Harlston released her, we both noticed how alert she looked and how quickly her tail wagged. Minutes after we opened the back door, she leapt out and walked towards the building on her hind legs. Harlston walked closely next to her, one hand in a pocket. I joined them.

'Listen,' she said, 'The Lord told me they would cry like this for me.'

'They're not doing it for you,' I told her, 'they don't have control over their actions.'

'Really?'

'Do you really know what we deal with?' asked Harlston, 'they're like you, only they take your form at night and aren't as talkative when in it.'

'I know them.'

'Yes,' said Harlston, 'Are they anything to do with your "Lord"?'

'They are,' she said, 'Soon they will be your masters. Take me to them.'

Harlston's response to this was a barely disguised laugh. 'What do you mean by masters?'

'The next step. The Lord's kind will rule the humans, and I will help it happen. And you are also helping it.'

'How are we helping it?'

'By bringing me to my disciples.' Having seen how she thought of the other patients, I decided not to let her see her "disciples" and instead escorted her to a secluded room, to her protest.

'Wait, I want to see them!' Her face became that frightening grimace again, which froze me but made Harlston get out his syringe.

'I don't think you are ready to see them just yet,' is what I told her.

'Perhaps. You will still talk to me though?'

'Of course.'

'I need you to help me learn about your world. I feel I still cannot understand it.'

'I intend to do just that,' I said as I led her to her room, 'Oh yes, do you have a name?'

'A name?' She looked at me surprised. 'I do not need a name.'

'I think you should have one though.'

'The Lord's is the only name I will need.'

I haven't told her, but I have named her Martha, after my mother. It is partly because of her I am doing this, after all.

After I made Harlston fetch some food for her, I took a look at her from outside the room. As I did, she stared at me, as if just doing that would bring me to her philosophy. Yet, there was a certain element of misery to her expression as well, as if she knew what she was really trapped in.

'When did you start hearing from this "Lord"?' I asked her.

'I always heard from him. I heard his voice when he moulded me, when he told me I was going to do great things. He said that this world needed to be started again as it wasn't good enough in its current state. He told me to get rid of those that were making things bad.'

'I've heard of you killing criminals.' As I asked her that, I took a look at her hands. Long bony fingers like spider legs, even a thumb, infected with straggly grey fur and with pads on the tips. Only her palms were free of hair.

'Those humans who hurt other humans? I had to. It's my purpose to get rid of them so we can be happier.'

'Do you really believe murder is the only option?'

'Are there other ways to make them go away?'

'We can put criminals in prisons, where...'

'So you won't get rid of them.'

'What?'

'They'll still be around. They won't be gone.'

'They won't hurt anyone if they are contained though.'

'I want a world completely free of people like them.' At that, she looked around at her surroundings. 'Wait. I am contained. You contained me.' She began to walk towards me. 'Do you think I'm a criminal?'

'No. No, I don't.'

'I don't think you're a criminal either.'

After I said that, I took out a gown from my quarters, pushed it through and asked if she could wear it. She stared at it for a few seconds, then picked it up and lifted it over her head. Fumbling around inside it, she soon found the largest hole and placed her head through it, before pushing her arms through the two other holes.

Harlston arrived with some meat which he quickly threw into Martha's room. She stared at it for a few seconds, and then began to devour it, clutching it tightly as she did so. Harlston watched her feast as closely as I did. 'When she's finished with that meal, I have some experiments I want to use her for.'

'It does seem somewhat soon.'

'It's never too soon. She may be the only way we can rectify our problem, after all.'

Harlston waited until Martha had finished her last piece of meat, and then grabbed her by the arms. Martha snarled and writhed in his grasp, but Harlston injected her, and after she calmed, he lifted her, and tied her down onto a table, suppressing those elongated appendages. I asked to accompany him, but he told me he would work better alone. Agreeing to his request, I decided to perform my routine nocturnal check, to see if there was still anyone who didn't succumb to their transformations.

During my check, I found that, while the majority of our patients had becoming the snarling beasts, Harold was still in his human form, yet screaming and punching the walls as he tried to suppress. I left him alone, as any interruptions, I feared, would cause him to succumb again.

After a while, I heard some odd footsteps, and then saw none other than Martha approaching me. I gasped at her appearance, but she too had an expression of shock on her face, which was bewildering to look at. The surprise that she gave left me unable to move, but I still tried to talk to her.

'What is the problem?'

'It's your friend. I don't like what he's been doing to me.'

'He is doing it for your own good.'

'But I don't like it. It's frightening.' She clutched me, like I was her mother. As she held me, I felt like I should have screamed, yet I couldn't bring myself to. By instinct, I attempted to pry her claws off my body. 'And...and...'

'Yes?'

Her expression grew more bewildering. 'Do you want to make me a human?'

I did not to answer, but instead escorted her back to her room. She didn't need any medication to calm her, and she walked beside me on all fours. She trusts me.

And I do want to make her human. I do want to make her what the Lord, not her Lord, intended her to be. I want to cure her and integrate her into our society, and do the same for all my patients. If she believes she has a mission from a higher force, so shall I.

7th January 1887

I am beginning to further regret our lack of funding, as I note the lack of surveillance for Martha's room. There is barely any money to hire someone, and I am beginning to doubt my associate.

When I walked to Martha's cell, I found her among her own faecal matter, childishly absorbed in it. She seemed to be trying to shape it into a model of some kind, and even smearing some of it in her own fur. Instantly, I was curious, but observed her for a few minutes. She seemed extremely focused, and didn't notice me watching her, until she turned around for a second. While her reaction to my viewing her wasn't too violent, I still found her growl most unnerving.

I enquired as to what she was doing, and she explained more of her religion. Faecal matter was apparently a potent material - she only referred to it as 'material' - for her brethren, and she explained how she remembered her god formed her from his own excretion. I asked her how, if the excretion only gains sentience when fully formed, she can remember her formation, and she only reminded me of the important role she is supposed to play in the future.

I then noted how human-like her attempts at sculpture appeared, and asked if she was trying to create life herself. 'This material is less potent than his, but it is perfect for making a shrine to him.' She continued with this act, and as she did, I ended up focussing on those strange hands of hers. Pausing for a moment, she added, 'Don't you make shrines to your God?' I saw this as an opportunity to explain my God to her to help her gain a greater comprehension of our world. I wasn't sure how much of it she'd believe, but at least I'd expand her knowledge.

'We do, but we...'

'And your God is dead.'

'What do you mean?'

'Everything dies, so your God must too.'

'No. He is eternal.'

'No. Nothing is eternal. He's dead.'

'So, is your god going to die too?'

'Yes, but he will die sooner if I don't do his work.'

'What will happen if he dies?'

'There will be no god. I must keep him alive until another one comes. There has been a long absence of a god before, and that's why there are so much bad things, and I'm keeping him alive by killing those bad people.' The way she explained this was oddly mechanical, and as she said those words, she never blinked. In a moment, she turned towards the cells of my other patients. 'They are helping keep him alive, and you want to kill them.'

'I do not wish to kill them. I am helping them with their conditions.'

'I've heard them. They hate the way they are.'

'And that's why I'm trying to help them.'

'You should help them embrace those conditions.'

This conversation reminded me of how she was unnerving the other patients, so I went off to calm them. I chose to visit Clentsworth first, as, despite him being new, I have not spoken to him much.

'Would you like to speak to me?' I asked him as I peeked through the window of his door.

There he sat, attempting to calm himself before turning to me. 'Yes.'

I kept outside his cell, worrying that entering would excite him. 'Have you been trying to repress?'

'I've tried, but I cannot. Can you help me?'

'Is there anything specific about your condition that you find troubling?'

He fidgeted.

'Please, tell me, I'm here to help you.'

After taking in a deep breath, Clentsworth continued, 'I've always felt I would die alone.'

'And when you became a werewolf...'

'It happened when I was trying to socialise...I went out into the forest with this girl I met...'

'Do you know where the girl is now?'

'I haven't seen her after it happened.'

'Still, you should not feel lonely. You are with me and Harlston, as well as others with your condition.'

'I think I should be alone, though.'

After we continued our discussion, which involved childhood as usual, I was approached by Harlston. 'Yes?' I asked him.

'I have been thinking,' he said, contemplatively, 'about Martha...'

'Yes, I've been meaning to talk with you about how you've been treating her.'

'She has such a deranged view on the world, so I'm not sure what I've been doing to her can really be called inhumane.'

'If it is torturous for her, then it is torturous. Now what do you want to tell me?'

'I've been thinking about her and our money problems. What if we charge people to come here and see her...'

I clenched my fists. 'You want to turn her into a sideshow attraction?'

'No, I think it would be good for her.'

'How?'

'You want her to join humanity, don't you?'

'I...do.'

'At the moment, I'm unsure if I can actually cure her condition, so surely more interaction with humanity can cause her and them to be friendlier with each other, and I believe she could, with the right treatment, be able to go out in public in her canine form.'

'She certainly isn't ready to interact with humanity right now. Every time I talk to her, she tries to draw me into her religion.'

'You don't believe that dribble, and I doubt the public will. These creatures prove our God, as they are creations of the Devil.' That was a belief I had held for quite a while, until I saw that exorcisms and prayer yielded no results. Our Mr. Gramson was a stern, religious man, and yet he continues to stay with us, and for all his prayer, he still can't suppress his transformation.

'I don't really think you care for her at all.'

'Why not consider my idea? I actually want people to be aware that her condition exists, rather than keep it a secret like you are.'

'The other patients want it to be kept a secret. And you do remember what happened to some of the people who found out.'

'Of course I do, but I don't believe all people will act that way. I daresay some may even see it as a good thing.'

I said nothing for a moment before responding. 'Remember how Mr. Cravver's wife reacted after she found out of his lycanthropy?'

'If you want to continue keeping these conditions a secret,' continued Harlston, 'I fear you may not be able to keep it a secret for very long. I have a sense that somehow everybody will find out. We do have an inspection tomorrow, and I am surprised they have not found out already.'

'Ah yes, I had forgotten about that.'

'I suppose we may have to show them Martha. And what will they do with her when they see her?' I took a moment to consider this, and began to fidget. 'I know the general behaviour of those in government. They'll take Martha away from us and put her in a circus.'

'But how is that any different from what you were suggesting?'

'If we let people see Martha, it will be for information purposes, not for...entertainment.'

'Please. Return to your work. I will try and settle something with Martha.'

'Very well,' replied Harlston, who walked away. His words drove me back to Martha's cell. While she seemed to be awake, she lay on the floor, still, framed by her artwork. All I had to do was call her, and she burst into life, rushing to the door and its miniature window.

'I was waiting for you.'

'There's a matter I need to discuss with you. We are having an inspection tomorrow, and I am...worried about what they make think of you.' Martha's energy disappeared as she slumped away from the window and crawled back to the middle of her cell. Then she turned her head in my direction.

'I think I know what you are talking about.' She gave a slight growl. 'The Lord told me about it. The humans are not ready yet.' She paused before walking towards the door again. 'I think you are though. The person who comes may be as well, if you know him.'

'I have doubts he will be.'

Her eyes bulged. 'You want me to hide?'

I didn't know how to answer.

'If you want me to hide,' she replied, stammering slightly, 'I will do so. I have been hiding for years, so I have had some practice.'

'Very well,' I told her, beginning to leave.

'No. Don't go.'

I found myself walking back to her door. 'What is it?'

'I heard you and that other man talking.'

'Did you?'

'Yes. I would like other humans to come and see me, but I can't.'

'Why?'

'The Lord says it is not time yet.'

'And when did he say this?'

'He said it just after the other man mentioned it.'

'His name is Harlston.'

'I prefer not to call him by a name. He doesn't deserve one.'

Both of us were silent.

'Have you any more to say to me?' said Martha, wagging her tail for a few moments.

'We will speak more about your religion tomorrow, but, I have other patients who need my aid and guidance.'

'You are the only man I can speak to now, and I hope to see you as much as I can. I will not be staying here long.'

'You will be seeing more of me,' I told her, slowly moving away from the door, 'but I have other business to attend. We'll talk more tomorrow after the inspection is finished.' With that, I walked away from the cell, leaving her alone with her thoughts. The sobbing from her room made me stand in the hall for a second, but the cries of Smertall made me continue.

Smertall had taken my advice and had gotten as much sleep as he could during the day to make it easier to control his nocturnal transformations, and had even requested we cover up his window with a thick curtain. He wanted to speak to me because while he was sleeping today, he had the most vivid nightmares. In the few hours of sleep I had managed to obtain, I have had some rather interesting dreams as well, so I tried to take heed of every word he said. He told me that as he slept, he dreamt of taking on his wolf form in daylight, completely aware of what he was doing, but still unable to control his actions. Then, another wolf entered through the door of his cell and told him to leave our institution and be free. Then he would run around a black abyss, until he sees a man he cannot identify before he wakes up.

I attempted to explain his dream. My theory was that he secretly felt some confidence in his wolf form, and his subconscious was telling him to embrace it. It was not uncommon among his kind, I told him, and I had every confidence in him to ignore that urge and continue fighting it.

After I left his cell, another theory appeared in my mind. What if Smertall's dream and what Martha has been telling me about are connected? That wolf from Smertall's dream could be...

No. If I believed that theory, it would mean that what Martha was talking about was true. And it is not. I aim to rid her head of such bizarre notions, and I will. Even if she may not physically become human, she should at least understand what the human world is truly like.

After my discussion with Smertall, I retired to my quarters for one of the few moments of sleep I allow myself, to help me consider my patients' stories better. I took off my jacket and lay down for a while on my sofa. It may not be comfortable, but it is my preferred way. My dreams may not be as lively as those of Smertall, but I swore I dreamt of his wolf, only I can't recollect exactly what it looked like.

My slumber took longer than I thought it would, but I awoke just before dusk. Seeing the lowering sun outside my window had me leap out of my chair and into the hallways, where the patients were already beginning to groan.

'Resist!' I told them, 'Remember what I have told you!' I couldn't think of anything else to say besides those things, but they inspired some of my patients. Some, but not all. Smertall once again held his head tightly, screaming, but managed not to transform when so many others did. The hallways had become a zoo, almost every cell holding a wolf. Each wolf howled, and Smertall fiercely grimaced at the howling.

Then came another howling. Martha's.

It was not the typical howling of a wolf, more like a human's bad impersonation of it. I suppose her unique anatomy had something to do with it.

Now that I consider it, it didn't sound like howling at all.

It sounded like a lullaby.

8th January 1887

The inspector arrived early the next morning, and, having not had any sleep the previous night, I was ready to welcome him. Harlston, however, was nowhere to be found. I had thought he was in his quarters, looking further into Martha, but I looked there, and saw no sign of him still.

Harlston may not have been experimenting, but that is still what I told the inspector when he entered the institution. The inspector was dressed entirely in black, as if he was attending a funeral, and seemed to blend in with his surroundings. I almost told him of our money troubles in hopes that it would make him more lenient, but I said nothing about it.

'You seem nervous,' said the inspector, lifting an eyebrow, 'Is there something I should know about?'

'No, there is nothing,' was my mere reply. The inspector said nothing in response except for a grunt. Both of us walked down the silent hallways, with the inspector breaking the silence.

'I smell something,' he told me, and I noticed we were nearing Martha's cell.

'It is one of our most recent patients,' I told him, 'She is a rather interesting case.'

The inspector shook his head. 'I understand. I find it strange how one could dabble in this for so long and yet still be surprised at what they find.'

'Indeed.'

A quick glance showed that Martha's cell was empty.

'We haven't released any patients recently,' I told the inspector, hoping he did not notice my twitching, 'but they are still making excellent progress.'

The inspection continued as it should have done. The stench of Martha's cell was never brought up again, and the conditions for the other cells were apparently fine. 'Everything seems in order,' he told me, 'Is there anything else you wish to discuss?'

'No, no, there isn't.' After sharing a few more words, I began to search the asylum for Martha. I did not ask any of the other patients if they had seen her, for fear of upsetting them. After searching the halls turned up nothing, I went outside to the gardens, feeling the damp air against my face.

In the snow-flecked greenery, I found both Harlston and Martha, just sitting there. When she turned around to see me, Martha laughed. It wasn't an insane laugh like those I am so accustomed to; it was a playful laugh, like that of a child.

'Oh, hello,' said Harlston, 'How did the inspection go?'

'Why are you two out here?'

'Well, I told you I was worried about what the inspector would think about her, so I took her out here.'

'I thought she didn't trust you.'

Martha approached me on all fours. 'He told me I could go outside though. I like the outside.'

'She is a wild animal,' Harlston told me, 'We can't keep her in that cell all the time.'

'She is not an animal, she is a human being. Furthermore, I am afraid of her being even a few centimetres from her room, considering what she has done outside these walls.'

Martha slouched down onto the grass, looking up at me with widening eyes. 'I told you, I did those things because I had to.' She sighed. 'I will go back if you want me to.' We stared at each other for a while before she entered the institution of her own accord.

'Fascinating little specimen, isn't she?' Harlston observed.

'I'm surprised you managed to make her trust you so quickly.'

'It probably has something to do with her "Lord". Did she not say we were instrumental to his goal of ruling the world?' I chose not to answer. 'Are you afraid of her?'

'She is something we haven't dealt with before.'

'That may well be, but working with werewolves and other supernatural things tend to lessen your sense of surprise. I knew she existed before beginning this career, and I've spent some of my time preparing myself for this inevitable meeting.' He began to pace around the gardens. 'I'm surprised you want to make her human actually. She's more interesting the way she is.'

'But have you been continuing your research on her?'

'Oh yes. It is too soon for anything groundbreaking, but I think there may be a very slight chance I could find a cure. I'm not sure I will be doing any research today though. I must look for those who need our help, and I think I have a friend who can aid us with our financial problems.' With that, he left.

After Harlston departed, I made my way towards Martha's room, where I saw she had returned there herself, and I locked the door behind her. As I did so, she looked up at me, still with that sad expression. 'Is something the matter?' I asked her, still trembling.

'I think you don't like me,' was her response.

'I am trying to help you.'

'I hope you are.'

'I am, and I do not wish for you to be uncomfortable, Martha.'

Her ears picked up, and she sprung to life. 'Did you call me something?' I had forgotten she had said she needed no name other than the Lord's.

'Yes,' I said, as I felt I had to be honest with her, 'I called you Martha.'

Her canine face twisted into a smile. 'You named me. You gave me a name. The Lord told me you would. You named me Martha. I am Martha.'

'Do you like that name?'

'Yes I do. It is a beautiful name. It proves you are special.'

I heard another patient scream. Gramson. He had been quite frantic recently, so I ran off to see what the problem was, but not before I took a minute to listen to Martha. She was talking, but not to me.

'He's named me. He's named me Martha. Thank you for bringing him me, Lord.'

1ˢᵗ February 1887

I am pleased to write down that Gramson, after having stayed with us for so many years, has successfully managed to suppress his nightly transformations, and today, he was released. Perhaps I shouldn't be so pleased; I will certainly miss his company, as he was quite an interesting person to have conversations with, and, since his family will no longer be supporting us, that may mean further financial troubles. They probably will find other werewolves and recommend us, but it is more likely they'll forget about us. So many people take so many things for granted in this age.

After I escorted him out of our institution to be reunited with his family, I noticed Martha's face pressed up against the window of her door, whining with wide eyes and another of her grimaces. When Gramson said his goodbyes, she was thrown into frenzy, not unlike the average patient at night. She howled, not like the wolf she resembled, she snarled, she ran around her cell, bouncing off walls. I had sadly made no progress with her the month she has stayed with us.

Knowing I wouldn't be able to talk with her in the state she was in, I instead turned my attention towards Harold Smertall. He has been succumbing to his transformations every day in the past week, and every time he tells me he'll do better, I find himself taking on his wolf form yet again. When I arrived at his room, I saw him lying on the floor in a foetal position, sobbing. I asked him what the matter was and he said it was Gramson leaving.

'It's...it's reminding me of how little willpower I have...' he told me, 'One night, I realised that as a wolf, I felt much freer, that...that all my cares seemed to go away. Recently, I've been thinking about Gertrude, but...but I don't as a wolf.'

'When you were a wolf, she was nothing but prey. Are you really saying you'd prefer to not care about people?'

'No, no I am not. Thinking about her and...I don't...really like it, so I just want some way to not think about it.'

'Those memories were why you came to us. I actually believe they are beneficial to your recovery. If you keep remembering what your wolf form is capable of, it will remind you to keep suppressing it. You have done a fine job of suppressing it in the past.'

'When I did suppress it,' he said, breathing heavily, 'I saw Gertrude's face staring right at me. She wouldn't stop staring. It's like...like she wanted me to transform.'

'I assure you,' I told him, placing a hand on his shoulder, 'She would not want you to transform again. If you truly want to honour her memory, you must suppress your wolf form.'

'I have tried. I have...' He began to sob again.

We spoke further, but our conversation went around in circles. No matter how much I told him to try harder at suppressing his transformations, he still wanted some time away from Gertrude. When he began to scream her name, I left the room as soon as possible. As I left Smertall to his own thoughts, I began to ponder what he told me. There are some things I do not enjoy thinking about, but I know I must think about them if I am to successfully run this institution and carry out what I intend to do. Sometimes I do wish these memories would vanish, but it would be foolish to live my life in denial.

After some rest to recover from Smertall's anxiety, I walked over to Martha's cell to see if she had calmed down. Fortunately, she was making no more noise, or running to and fro. Instead, she sat quietly in the centre of her room, giving me a stern look as I approached her.

'Hello!' I said, 'Are you in a mood to talk?'

'You sent away one of my disciples.'

'Do you mean Gramson?'

'Why did you make him go away?'

'Because...we have done everything we can for him.'

Her face started to lighten up. 'So he is ready to spread my word? Did you tell him what I told you?'

I said nothing.

'I wanted to talk with him.' Her eyes narrowed, her face taking on that angry glare again. 'Why didn't you let me talk to him?'

'I wasn't sure they were ready. I thought you may upset them.'

'They are ready. They are like me. Let me talk to them.'

'Are you sure?'

'I don't have much time left here. I must talk to someone,' she said. Before I could respond, she came closer. 'I remember you said something about a man named Harold. You said you were worried. Let me talk to him.'

'I am afraid he is not in the state to talk to anyone.'

'If you are worried about him, let me talk to him. I will help him. The Lord wants me to.'

Unable to think of a response that would appease her, I began to turn around, and noticed Harlston standing right behind me.

'Why are you here?' I asked Harlston.

'You say Smertall is beginning to feel comfortable in his wolf form,' Harlston observed, 'I think that what he needs is proof of how hideous such a thing is. Just imagine how he would feel about his less civilised form if he saw what it has done to dear Martha.'

'I do not want to bring him here to talk to her...'

'He is not the first person to gain this odd comfort from being a werewolf, and I believe Martha is the best example of how this condition can warp one's mind. If we don't want him to succumb to the form, we must make him fear it.'

After some consideration, I decided, if I alone was not going to get far with Smertall, we would attempt a conversation with Martha to see how he reacts to it. After he had taken a rest from his sobbing, we strapped him to a table and wheeled him over to Martha's cell, making him close enough to talk to her and her to talk back.

'I sense one of my own,' we heard Martha say as she pressed her face against the window of her door. After I untied some of his straps, Smertall lifted himself to look at her. 'Hello,' she said, 'I am Martha. I am here to talk to you.'

Smertall clenched his teeth together, attempting to say something.

'I hear you are uncomfortable with your gift,' said Martha.

Smertall forced words out of his mouth. 'G...gift.'

'You are helping everyone towards the next step. The world will be better and the people will be better. You and I and everyone here will be the start of it. The Lord will rule, and all will be wolves.'

'NO!' The table shook. 'Don't mock me!'

Harlston interrupted. 'Have you ever met Mr. Smertall before?'

'No, I have not.'

'He tells us he gained his condition on a hunting trip, and since you are so outgoing, I thought...'

'I have seen hunters. They kill my food for amusement. If I had met him when he was hunting, I would have killed him.' A growl escaped her throat before she resumed. 'You should be glad you have your gift. You will become a better person.'

'G...Gertrude...'

'Who is Gertrude? Is she another wolf?'

'No. I killed her...because of my gift.'

'It was probably because she was not needed in the Lord's new world.'

Screaming, Smertall thrashed back and forth on his table before we strapped him down again. 'I couldn't help myself. I tried to stop myself but I couldn't...'

'I have heard of this. You only become a wolf at night, and have no control. I think I will have the Lord help me with this.'

Leaping away from the window, she moved to the centre of her cell. She sat silent, and for a few minutes, the only sound to be heard was Smertall's heavy breathing.

'Are you not going to greet the Lord?'

Smertall's body began to tremble again. 'Why?'

'He is right next to me.' She still sat in her cell, alone. 'Oh no. I think only I can see him and hear him. I was hoping you could, but I don't think you can. I will tell you what he says though.' Once again, she moved to the door. 'You are worried about being mindless when you are a wolf.'

'Yes.'

'The Lord says he has a solution.'

'He does?'

'Yes. He says you can become like me.'

'What?'

I interjected. 'How?'

She paused, and turned behind her. 'He said I should figure it out,' she said, before walking around her cell in deep thought. 'People can be made into night wolves by being bit by another,

I have heard. Maybe if I bite you, I can make you like me, always a wolf, never mindless.'

'No...' Tears streamed from his eyes again.

'The Lord says I should.'

'Do not listen to the Lord!' Harlston cried, 'He is not what you think he is!'

'Harlston!'

'He is a demon, taking advantage of your condition and leading you astray! If you continue to listen to him, you will be damned!'

'Don't say that about the Lord!' hissed Martha, 'He is not happy about it!'

'I have seen him before,' continued Harlston, breathing as loudly as Smertall, 'and he has done this with everyone he has come into contact with. He is a liar, a villain, and listening to him will spell your doom! He must be cast out!' Taking a step back, Harlston pulled out a crucifix from his pocket. 'I cast you out in the name of our true Lord Jesus Christ! Leave this place and never return! Your power is worthless against that of the true God!' He took two steps forward, still holding out the crucifix. 'It's working! He is getting weaker! Fear not, Martha, you will be free!'

'The Lord is not weaker.'

'He is! He is being cast out in the name of Christ!'

'He is laughing at what you are doing.' With that, Harlston stopped and relaxed his arms. 'What you just did was insulting to him, but I know you will submit to him soon.'

'Martha, he is a lie!' That comment made Martha try to reach for Harlston with one of her claws, or arms, I am still unsure what to call them. Harlston took a step back, and then grabbed Martha's arm. Then he unleashed a needle and jabbed her with it. It did nothing to calm her. While Harlston stayed, I wheeled back Smertall to his room.

'Thank you...' he wheezed as I released him from his straps.

'I apologise if I made you distraught.'

'You did not, but she certainly did,' he told me. Sitting down, he sighed and buried his face in his hands.

'Do you wish to talk to me about it?'

'No.' I walked out of the room and closed the door as Smertall began shaking his head. 'No, I don't want to talk about it. Please, leave.'

'Very well then, I will leave you alone if you wish me to. However, if you feel disturbed again, do not hesitate to call me and I will discuss anything with you.'

'Leave.'

I did as he commanded before I ran into Harlston again. 'Did you mean to excite Martha like that?' We walked side by side as we spoke.

'I was merely experimenting with a trick I had used before. I have met many patients who claim to be possessed by demons, and false exorcisms like that usually help them on their way to recovery.'

'She doesn't believe she is possessed,' I said, moving closer, 'She believes our God is dead and her Lord is *the* Lord.'

'That still means she believes in God. Perhaps what I told her will at least make her reconsider her beliefs.' He put his finger to his chin. 'But maybe she does have a point...'

'I have tried to introduce her to the Word. I have read the Bible to her about every day for the last two weeks, and she still refuses it.'

'Yes. There are some who may say her religion makes as much sense as ours.'

I moved away from his face and began to pace around the halls. 'What was that you injected her with?'

'That? Ah yes.' After Harlston said that, he led me into his study. I know full well I should be monitoring his experiments, yet I rarely enter his room. The body parts and the wolf foetuses may unnerve some, but I find a comfort in this room; it reminds me something is being done. 'It is based on something I have been working on ever since I took this position,' Harlston continued, picking up some notes from his desk. 'I have been interested in how werewolves spread their curse to humans and I have been trying to replicate it.'

I stared at the notes he held. 'Why would you do it?'

'I wondered if, some day, we might consider turning ourselves into werewolves to better understand how their minds work. Also, perhaps it would help make a cure.'

'I am certain we can understand their minds without becoming them ourselves. Why would you give such a thing to Martha?'

'You did want her to be human, did you? To be able to go out into public?'

'Yes.'

'Well, I am unsure I can make her fully human right now, but I believe I can transform her into a regular werewolf. She may be a wolf by night, but by day, she will be...*look* human.' He began to pace about his room. 'It is obvious how she got her condition,' he continued, glancing at a diagram on his wall about the anatomy of humans and wolves, 'The werewolf curse can be inherited from birth. So if someone can be born as both a wolf and a human, a birth defect can cause one to be a combination of both species. And since Martha is already a combination of wolf and human, it shouldn't be too difficult to separate the two.' His pacing became quicker. 'And, if I compare my notes on her current status with those of the form I will give her, I could find a way to isolate her human side. And if I fail to do that and she stays a normal werewolf, with our help, maybe she too could repress the transformations.'

'And what you injected her with will make that happen?'

'I am unsure it will have any effect on her right now. If it does not, I will continue to tweak the formula until I get results.'

I stood a few moments in silence, scratching the back of my neck. 'I will continue to let you continue with this experiment, but only for use on Martha. If you turn me or yourself into a werewolf, I will decide your services will no longer be required.'

'Very well,' said Harlston, 'I shall return to my experiments. And I am sorry, but I will require some privacy for them' He shoved me out of his study, leaving me to stand in the halls to go over my thoughts.

What Harlston did while we were visiting Martha reminded me of a mental image I had when I was taking care of her. I have been imagining what her Lord may look like, and my picture of him was a gigantic demonic wolf, standing on all fours, towering above the whole institution. As he arrived, all the patients were either screaming in terror or cheering. Martha just stood there, her head held high. With a single roar from the Lord, Martha suddenly shuddered in fear. I, somehow, defeated the Lord, perhaps using the power of God like Harlston prepared to do, or battled him. The Lord disappeared, curing all my patients of their conditions. Martha would be free of her wolf form and become a beautiful woman, thanking me for freeing her.

Just a power fantasy. It is childish of me to think such things, actually. Perhaps that's all what Martha says is. She has been overpowered by the world and wishes for some higher force to change things to her favour. I have seen things like this before, and will undoubtedly encounter more cases of it. All I have to do is snap Martha out of her delusion, and she should be on her way to humanity.

After attempting to get as much sleep as I could, I woke up just in time to check on the patients and help them resist their nocturnal metamorphosis. The first room I checked was Martha's. She was standing on her hind legs, muttering to herself. Harlston's formula had no effect.

I left her, then returned to the other patients, reminding them to suppress. Once again, most of them became growling wolves, all except Harold. I saw him in his room, clenching his teeth, sweat dripping down his face. Harlston may have had a point, but I am still unsure about being a fear-monger.

Although I suppose sometimes fear is utterly necessary for redemption.

8th February 1887

Harold Smertall has been making excellent progress suppressing his transformations, and I have not seen him take on his wolf form for an entire week. Once again, I found myself contemplating releasing him, but like the last time, he may begin succumbing again. Then there is the fact the catalyst for his resistance is Martha and her stories.

I have been receiving letters from his wife, asking when he will be coming home. I once wrote to her saying I was strongly considering it, only to write to her again saying he still was succumbing. I received another letter from her yesterday, filled with more questions concerning his release. Here, she made clear to note she fully forgave him for Gertrude, and that she would have wanted him to move on.

I read the letters out loud to Smertall, as I always do when I receive them. 'Do you really think,' he asked me, 'that Gertrude would want me to forgive myself?'

'Of course.'

'When I've been trying to resist,' he said, looking around his room, 'I keep telling myself that, but sometimes...I see her walking down the hall...'

'And then?'

'I tell her to go away. She is not Gertrude...she isn't...she's that...'

'You were resisting the change because of Martha?'

'No. I'm resisting it because I want to. I'm not comfortable in that wolf form anymore.'

I then started to discuss a release with him. I suggested, if he manages to repress his nightly transformations for at least another week, that he go back home to his wife for a few days, just to see how it would suit him. If he continued to conquer his need to transform, he could stay home, but if anything happened, he would return to our institution. I even suggested arrangements for his wife to go out at night to make sure she wouldn't get hurt if the transformation does occur. He agreed to this arrangement.

Yesterday, Harlston, after tweaking the formula a bit, had injected Martha again. Today, I decided to check on her to see if there was any change. When I arrived, she was pacing around her cell on her hind legs, still in that hybrid form. Seeing her pace reminded me that it had been a while since I had spoken to her. I don't why I have neglected to further discuss things with her; perhaps I realised that it would be futile to try and stop her worshipping her Lord, or maybe I thought she would realise how insane her delusions were on her own.

'Hello,' she said, her face peering from her door's window.

'I wish to talk to you, if that is fine with you.'

'It is fine with me,' she said, a slight smile on her snout. 'May I ask you something though?'

'Very well.'

'May you come in?'

I didn't reply. Could I really go into a small room with our only patient that willingly kills? Who constantly tried to convert me to her cause? Her very bite could make me one of hers.

'Are you going to come in?'

I paced like she had been doing earlier, thinking of her fangs and how she could dig them into my flesh. What if I was not needed anymore for her scheme, and she was ready to slice me to pieces?

As she watched me, her eyes narrowed. 'Are you?'

Refusing her request would only make her more furious, so I opened the door slightly, quickly slipped in, and slammed it behind me. She would not get out of this room; she would stay here, alone, with me.

I stared at her long, twisted smile.

When I entered, the stench of her faecal matter clenched to my nostrils, intensifying Martha's presence. After looking over me, she walked to the back of the room, still smiling.

'I am not sure I can stay long,' I said to her, pressing against the door, 'I have business to do.'

Her fangs.

'Please stay as long as you can.' Her smile grew shorter. 'I think you are my friend, and I like to talk to you.'

My hand still neared the door handle. 'Is there anything you want to talk about?'

Straightening herself up, Martha replied. 'Yes.' Before she continued, she walked closer to me, not very much though. 'Do you have a dog?'

'No,' I replied quietly. 'Do you want a dog?'

'Yes. I have met some before I came here, and they made me feel comfortable. I miss them now.'

It makes sense that a canine should find comfort in other canines, and I should probably fulfil her request, just to see how the two would react to each other. It would also probably explain some of her behaviour. With her, almost anything is worth trying.

'Martha,' I asked her, 'Before you came here, did you feel oppressed?'

Her ears pricked up as her face warped. 'Oppressed?'

'Did you feel people were trying to be better than you?'

'I have seen lots of people who thought they were better. The Lord told me he didn't like them, so I had to get rid of them.'

My hand now clenched the handle tightly, but my arm was frozen. 'I...I believe you are upset by how people have been treating you...and that you wished to be better than them, so you made the Lord in your mind to give yourself a sense of importance.'

'I did not create the Lord. The Lord created me. I cannot create something that created me.'

'What I am saying is that you imagined the Lord creating you, because...' My fingers drummed against the handle. '...have you ever felt helpless? Have you ever felt scared?'

Martha walked to a corner of her room and sat still. 'I have felt scared. Sometimes this place makes me feel scared.'

'When you are scared, do you think about the Lord?'

'Yes, I do. When the Lord has his way, places like this will go away. Everywhere will be bright and green. It will always be warm and never cold. We will all be free.'

'Do you think this world can really be achieved by killing people?'

'It gets rid of people who could stop it from happening. I don't think you will stop it from happening, so I won't kill you.'

My leg twitched. 'I would like a world like that too.'

'I know you would. I know you don't like being here.' Do I? 'That is why you named me.'

'Yes, I did name you.'

She moved closer to me, and I did nothing to stop her. 'Why did you name me Martha? It is a lovely name, but where did it come from?'

The muscles in my arms and legs loosened, and I sighed. 'It was the name of my mother. Do you remember having a mother?'

She raised her head and began to ponder. 'I think I know what a mother is. It is a woman that cares for people.'

'That is a suitable description, I think.'

'I am a mother. I am a mother to all these wolves here. I love them and I will care for them.'

'Do you remember being cared for by a woman?'

She stood for a moment before answering. 'No, no, I don't remember.' Her smile was gone.

'Do you want me to tell you about my mother?'

Martha, on all fours, crawled away from me. 'Tell me if you want to.'

I breathed in heavily, readying myself. Though if I were to tell anyone about this, it might as well be her. 'My mother was a werewolf. She became one when I was very young. She went out at night with my father, and got attacked.'

'She only became a wolf at night?'

'Of course.'

'I wonder what that would be like.' She placed a claw to her snout and looked away from me. 'I keep hearing about it, but have never had it happen to me.'

'On her first transformation, she almost...she almost killed my father, and when she found out, she...' I turned around and my face pressed hard against the door.

'What did she do?' I heard Martha say.

I breathed in. I breathed out. My mother...her soft face, or at least, what I remember of it, flashed in my mind. 'She killed herself.' My hand clenched the handle again.

'So she is dead.' I didn't face her when she said that, but I imagined those words coming from my mother's mouth.

'Yes, she is dead.'

Another growl came from Martha. I left and slammed the door behind me, making sure to lock it. Her growls sounded more animalistic than usual as she leapt off the walls, and walked around as if stalking some prey. Before I left her by herself, I heard the most unusual sound from her room.

I heard crying.

'Lord...so many of your people have died...if they die, you will die...I will not let you die...'

9th February 1887

I have been losing so much sleep recently. It may mean I have been less focussed, and my mind has wandered, but at least I am able to observe the patients during their nightly transformations more easily. Smertall continues to repress his metamorphosis, and even appears to be having less trouble doing so. When I saw him, I wondered if the human mind alone could cure the werewolf condition. Than I had a thought that the condition could be completely due to the mind; the victim believes they are a wolf so strongly that their body twists and turns to suit that way of thinking. Martha strongly wanted to be a talking wolf, so her mind and body worked in unison to make it true. I am aware that this theory was a completely ludicrous one. It is just one I wanted to be true.

Maybe if I believe it to be true hard enough, it would be.

Today, Harlston, having thought over what I told him about Martha, fulfilled her request and brought in a dog. A mutt. Its scraggled fur matched that of Martha's, though its eyes were duller than hers.

'Are you sure this is a good idea?' I asked him.

'Of course. You do want your patients to be comfortable, do you not? If this will make her more comfortable, we should do it.'

'How do you know that dog will be safe with her? She might kill it.' I wanted to add that she may make it a werewolf, or make it anthropomorphic, as those thoughts struck my mind at that moment. Thankfully, I restrained myself from saying those things.

'You are far too paranoid. She only killed those people because she thought they were 'bad'. We are her friends, so she is as meek as a kitten. Similarly, I am certain she won't think this creature has any malevolent intent.' Dangling from

Harlston's grasp, the dog looked around with large, watery eyes as Harlston spoke.

'Where did you find that dog? You realise we do not have the funds...'

'I found him. He is a stray. I am aware of hygienic concerns, but this is the type of dog Martha would be most familiar with.' I would have said something, but I am certain he would not have listened to me. 'Oh yes, and I feel I am doing well with my serum. It should be completed by next month.'

I followed him to Martha's cell, where she looked out of her window to catch a gaze at what Harlston had for her. She may have smiled as widely as ever, but the mutt squirmed in Harlston's arms as it saw her, barking. Despite the creature's protests, Harlston threw it into the cell and left it with Martha. Peering through the window, I was reminded of when I was in that room yesterday.

Dogs are usually terrified of wolves. The mutt followed this tradition, cowering to a corner of the cell as Martha approached it, the latter bearing her row of unnatural teeth. When she approached the mutt, she began to sniff it in greeting. After a few seconds of this, the mutt followed suit, and soon both of them were getting acquainted with each other's scent. Soon, Martha stroked through the mutt's fur with her elongated paw, with the dog lying down and wagging its tail.

'You really should listen to me more,' said Harlston, his long nose in the air, 'I know what is best for these creatures, as you can see here. And,' he continued, with that smirk he is known to have, 'I am still contemplating having paying people arrive here to observe her and the other patients.'

I turned away from the playful wolf and sighed at Harlston. 'I can't believe you are still thinking of exploiting her.'

'It would not be exploitation, it would be charity. All of our profits will be used to fund and improve our institution. I really do want people to stop taking things like this for granted.'

'I know you wish to exploit her...'

'No, I wish for more people to know about her. Such a beautiful, rare creature like her should be shown to the world. Everyone should know about her, and should learn not to be afraid of her. Look at her with that dog.' I peered through the window, and saw Martha rubbing the mutt on the stomach, the dog's leg kicking the air. 'The people fear a bloodthirsty monster is out and about ready to kill them, so to see that malevolent creature in this state will surely soothe their fears.' He moved his face closer to mine, and smiled. 'They'll know her better, and she'll have some human interaction; it will benefit so many.'

'I am still unsure,' I replied, making his smile vanish, 'If we introduce Martha to the general public, it would really be no different than having her in a circus. The media would never stop talking about this, and I fear that giving Martha publicity like that would fuel her delusions.'

'Certainly if she spoke to more people she would realise how foolish her beliefs are on her own.'

'The purpose of this institution,' I said, my eyelids lowering, 'is to make sure these werewolves are given the chance for a normal life. Martha was not meant to be like this, she was meant to be human, and I intend to rectify this mistake.'

'Very well. I will continue to modify the serum until I am sure I can make her a regular werewolf, then I could try and find a way to make her fully human, if that is what you desire. I am not one to defy his superiors.' Before he left, he took one more look at Martha and her new friend.

15th February 1887

Another week has gone by, and Smertall has not transformed at night. In fact, while most of the other patients have been howling, he has been sitting in his cell rather calmly. So, this morning, his wife has arrived here to take him home. She waited outside the main entrance, as she did not wish to witness others with her husband's condition.

Harlston was once again nowhere to be found, so I alone greeted Smertall as he slowly awoke. I told him his wife was outside, and his only response was 'Good.' After he crawled out of his room, I took him by the hand and escorted him through the halls. As I did so, I thought about how I would miss him if he did not return. He had been with us for many months, and I had almost thought of him as a friend, given how much he was willing to share with me.

As we walked down the hallway, we passed by Martha's cell, and she had her face peering out to watch us. We heard her mutt bark.

'Do you want to say goodbye, Martha?' Since I still believe Martha helped Smertall repress his monster, I thought she should have one last conversation with him.

'Yes,' she said, 'but we will see each other again.'

Smertall said nothing to this, and I am glad he did not.

'If we find a permanent cure,' I said to Smertall as we passed Martha's cell, 'I will let you know as soon as possible.'

'Thank you.'

Those were the last words I heard from him before he was reunited with his wife, who embraced him with a tight hug. I watched them as they spoke of each other and Gertrude, and as they walked away back to their safe, secure home. I stood outside even as they left, hoping that more of my patients would have this opportunity. As I entered, Smertall's absence already began to sting. When he and Gramson were here, their potential for recovery gave this place an iota of light, it helped keep me doing this. Now that they are gone, the patients remaining are Martha and werewolves who have little to no willpower. I do not have many conversations with Mr. Enfeld or Mr. Clentsworth, because they usually do not wish to speak to me. It seems the only reason they are here at all is to contain them when they transform.

Sometimes I think that this institution is merely a place to keep werewolves so they don't attack people any more, even though we have had a few patients leave the halls. Some of our patients have been here for years, and still show no sign of improvement.

I considered revisiting Enfeld's and Clentsworth's cases, to see if there was any chance they could suppress their transformations, but at the moment, I had not the will to speak to anyone regarding their conditions or mental states. Instead, I sat on a chair in the hallway, and tried thinking about nothing. I needed to relax; it was my own little reward for taking care of Smertall.

As I sat down, I heard the squeaking of wheels coming down the hall, and rose from my seat to see what the noise was. Harlston had Mr. Enfeld strapped to a table and was wheeling him down the halls. I did not need to ask what he was doing. Since he thought talking with Martha had helped Smertall with his condition, it would do the same for others. While feeling irritated that he did something like this without my permission, I followed him, saying nothing as I did so.

When we arrived at Martha's room, she peeked through the window as she usually did. 'Thank you.'

Enfeld peered up as best as he could. 'I've heard of you.'

'I know.'

Briefly trying to break his restraints, Enfeld snarled. 'Don't mock me.'

Martha was taken aback. 'Mock?'

'You're laughing at me. That's what you're doing.'

Her face scrunched up. 'No. I don't want to make you unhappy. I want to make things good.'

'Don't talk to me like you're my mother.'

'I am your mother.'

That response caused Enfeld to release a torrent of laughter. 'You are mocking me.'

Martha shrunk at the sound of Enfeld's laughter. 'But I'm trying to help you.'

'You can't help me. You can't, and neither can these two. I *have* to transform at night, and there's nothing I can do about it. Everyone here is having a laugh at me about it, especially you.'

'How am I mocking you?'

'Look at you. You're always in that form yet you can keep your sense...'

Martha sprung to life again. 'Oh. I can make you like me, if that is what you want. All I have to do is bite you, and you can keep your sense all the time.'

'I'd actually like you to do that,' said Enfeld, shaking in an attempt to be free of his restraints. 'Come on, untie me, let her bite me.'

I saw Harlston's fingers near Enfeld's straps, and grabbed him by the wrist. 'We can't do this!'

'I think it would be worth it, just to see if it does have any effect. I haven't been able to replicate her bite after all.'

'No, I won't...'

'It's very possible her bite will have no effect. Still, I think this would be necessary in studying her.'

My hand still grabbing Harlston's wrist tightly, I pulled his hand away from the restraints, and caused him to stumble over. At this, Enfeld began to laugh again, and Harlston wheeled him back to his room. The laughter still echoed, and it made Martha crawl away from the window, and towards her mutt.

'Don't worry,' she said to her dog, stroking its fur, 'He will listen to me. I know he will.'

16th February 1887

Since that meeting yesterday seemed to have upset Martha
somewhat, the first thing I did this morning was talk to her.
She wanted to go outside to the gardens, assuring me she
would not attack or bite me or anyone else if she did. Since the
last time she went out caused no harm, I unlocked her door, let
her out and led her to the gardens. It was still cold, but with the
snow cleared up, the hedges and flower bushes flourished, and
thus, Martha drew her attention towards them. I hope to fulfil
any of her requests that have no potential for harm, just to
assure her that I want to treat her like a human being rather
than an animal.

Her mutt joined us for the miniature outing, loyally following
Martha as she followed me. I find myself rarely going outside,
so the grey sky and the damp, cold air were made all the
worse. Not minding the weather one iota, Martha stretched her
legs and ran around the gardens. Close behind her was her
mutt, joyfully panting. They raced about in circles, until both
were tired and lay down near a bush.

'Is there anything else you want to talk to me about?' I asked
her as she tried to catch her breath.

'There is,' she replied, her mouth revealing those teeth, 'Why
wouldn't you let me bite that man?'

'I was afraid, that since he is so flustered about his condition
already, that making him like you would make him worse.'

'But he said he wanted it.'

'I was worried it would be a decision he would regret...'

'William thinks I should have done it.'

'William?'

She gestured her head towards her mutt, cuddling close to her
for comfort.

'Far be it for me to disagree with him,' I said, 'but it may not be time for him to become like you.'

'Maybe it is not,' said Martha, stroking her dog, 'But last night, the Lord told me his time would be soon.'

'How soon?'

'He didn't say. He often doesn't tell me things.' After she said that, she turned away from her dog and walked, on her hind legs, towards a bench. She didn't sit down on the bench, rather just place a paw on it. 'Do you believe that the time will come when people will not fear me?'

I approached her. 'Of course. Aren't you certain the Lord will have his way?'

'I sometimes am certain,' she said, 'but now I'm beginning to think the Lord may die after all.'

'Why is that?'

'Sometimes when I talk to him, he seems quite weak. One time, he was very angry at me for not letting my message get across to that Gramson person. He said that if I don't do my work well, he will punish me.' Instantly after those words, she ran to the door, only to find I had locked it. 'Please open this door. I want to talk to Enfeld again.'

'He does not take you seriously, so speaking to him would be futile.'

'I think if I speak to him, he will believe. And I promise I won't bite him.'

'I think it will be better if you don't interact with him. He doesn't like you, and you may make him excited.'

Saying nothing, Martha walked from the door on all fours and looked up at the sky. 'I like the outdoors.'

'So do I.'

'I have walked around a lot,' she said, 'I have been exploring the world, because that is what the Lord told me to do.'

'Did you like exploring?'

'Yes,' she replied, turning to her dog and then to me, 'except nobody would listen to me.'

I stroked her fur like she stroked that of William. As my fingers reached upwards for her neck, I felt a number of scars on her body. Claw marks. 'You are not alone. I sometimes feel that way too.'

'That is a shame,' she replied, 'I think you are very wise.'

'It is good to hear someone does.'

At that moment, the door opened, revealing Harlston. 'Ah, there you are!' The door still wide open, he walked towards us, smiling all the while.

Martha darted in. Her dog sat still.

'You fool! She'll be after Enfeld!'Both of us ran after her, and saw her already sitting outside Enfeld's door. We made no movement.

'Oh ho ho, it's you again. Who let you off your leash?'

'Don't be like that. I'm here to tell you about the Lord.'

'Oh yes, I've had people tell me about 'the Lord'. Some've thought I'm 'evil' for not going to church and all that. Well, if God is so great, why hasn't he stopped me ending up like this?'

'Because God is dead. I am talking about the Lord who gave you that gift.'

'You're off your rocker. But I suppose that's why you're here.'

Harlston crept closer to Martha, trying not to make any noise, reaching for a syringe from his coat pocket.

'Hey!' Enfeld came closer to the window of his door. 'What about that offer to make me like you?' He stuck his arm out of the window. 'That still good?'

Carefully Harlston lifted his syringe.

'Hello, Harlston!' Martha turned around, her face and her voice filled with an odd cheer. 'Would you like to join us?'

All need for subtlety had vanished. Once again I began to run, almost falling over as I did so.

Martha's fangs dug into Enfeld's arm.

When I saw this, I seized the syringe from Harlston's clutch, and struck it into Martha's neck. The second she began to feel drowsy, I lifted her back to her cell and closed the door, not even caring about her mutt. 'How could you let this happen, Harlston?'

'Don't get so upset,' he told me, standing still with eyes on Enfeld, 'Her bite likely won't have any effect on him. If it does, my serum should be ready soon, and will deal with both his and her little problem. Not completely, of course...'

'I really do hope you are still working on that serum,' I said, 'it is the only reason I'm still keeping you.'

'I actually think without me,' Harlston replied, his mouth curving upwards, 'our situation would be far worse. I have a good mind to resign right now, just so my absence can make you can appreciate me better.'

'Hubris is the last thing we need around here.'

'On the contrary,' said Harlston, hands behind his back, 'that, as well as a firm backbone, are necessary to work in a place like this.'

20th February 1887

The day after Martha bit Enfeld, I checked up on him, and saw him human. Since werewolf infections are usually instantaneous, and the sounds coming from Enfeld's throat did sound disappointed, I took this to mean that Martha's bite really did have no effect, and I left him alone. He was usually in no mood to talk to me, so I left him alone for a while. I also left Martha alone for a couple of days; perhaps it would help her realise that what she did was wrong.

Today though, Harlston told me Enfeld wanted to talk to me, which he rarely wanted to do, so I went over to his room right away. As I walked over, I swore I heard laughter coming from Martha's room, and dismissed it as her playing with William.

'Hello there, doctor,' said Enfeld, his voice slightly lower, 'I've been waiting for you.'

When I heard the tone he spoke in, I instantly suspected it, but tried to tell myself it couldn't be. Still I peered into the cell, and saw him now covered in scraggly fur, his clothes looser, his face twisted into a row of jagged teeth. Seeing this, I closed my eyes and turned away.

'I'm very sorry, Enfeld...'

'Don't be sorry,' he said with a growl, 'I actually quite like this. You never really appreciate the form until you have control in it. It's...different.'

Stumbling away, I attempted to respond. 'You actually like that form?'

'Yes, at least I can get a good night's sleep in it. I probably would enjoy it even more if you let me out.'

At that moment, I forced myself to look at him. As I forced myself to stare straight at his deformed face, I swear I heard whispers from within his room. 'I can't do that.'

'Come on. I'm not going to kill anyone. I may show it off a bit, though.'

'Don't you know how people may react to it?'

'I'll probably end up in a sideshow or something, but it'll be better than this place.'

As I stared into his new animalistic eyes, Harlston arrived. 'Do you want to talk to Martha at all?' he asked.

'Yeah, I would,' he said, smiling her smile, 'Then perhaps I could show her how to really use a body like this.' He unleashed his new claws.

'Oh dear,' said Harlston.

'Now look what you have done,' I said to Harlston, grabbing him by the shoulders.

'This wasn't my doing, it was Martha!'

'She had no control over it, you let her do this!'

Enfeld laughed that laugh, making us both silent. 'Do you know why I didn't resist my transformations at night? Because it felt too good. Now...it's always going to be good.'

22nd February 1887

The more Enfeld stays in that anthropomorphic form, the more he seems to get comfortable in it. When I come to check up on him, I see him swiping away at invisible prey, chomping away at his meals like it was a fresh kill, and attempting a howl.

Today, I arrived to his room to talk to him. He spoke before I did, 'Let me out.'

I said nothing.

'I said, let me out.'

I still remained silent.

'Are you afraid?'

'No, I am keeping you here for your own benefit.'

'I think it would "benefit",' he said, 'if you let me out. I want to go out. I want to be a wild animal, I want to be free.'

'You are not an animal.'

'I am now, aren't I? I've heard so much about the life animals have, hunting, fighting to survive, and I thought about it to myself last night. That's the type of life I'd like, and I suppose you'd want a life like that too, wouldn't you?'

'Why do you think I'd like a life like that?'

'You run this place, don't you? Just you and Harlston?'

'Yes.'

'It must be pretty hectic, taking care of us. Wouldn't you prefer to be free?'

Would I like to be free? Free of the cacophony of howling at night? Free of the responsibility of keeping a secret that had to be kept? I've wished I was free of all this, yet I know that the only way for me to be free of it is if it just disappeared. There is no way I know of that I can make it disappear, and if I give this up, there would be so many who wouldn't be free of this.

'It would be so great, wouldn't it? To just say goodbye to all this shit. I actually think these folk would be better off without you. They'd feel better just turning into wolves than constantly being told not to.'

'It may not feel better, but some of these patients hate what has happened to them, and I'm trying to help them face their curses better.'

'I once thought what happened to me was a curse,' he said, 'but now I've realised it has its advantages. Maybe I should thank you.'

'Why?'

'I didn't really realise there was a good point to all of this until I came here. It wasn't my idea, but now I'm actually glad I came.' He smiled that smile yet again. 'Maybe I'll repay you somehow.'

When he gave his thanks, I could no longer bear to keep looking at him, and walked away. As I walked back to my quarters, I pondered what it would be like to be an animal. I have read several books about the behaviour of wolves, and though the facts I read about those creatures rarely apply to my patients, they are most interesting. What would it be like to be part of a pack, following the orders of an alpha male, having to constantly battle lesser beasts for sustenance? I am not one for thrills, an odd thing to say in this position, but I still wonder what it would be like to be free of troublesome emotions like misery and regret. Perhaps Mother did not fully know what she had been given.

Enfeld is an animal. He acted like one when he first came here, so this fate is a most fitting one. This institution *is* nothing more than containment. Enfeld shouldn't go among human society, and neither should Martha. I and Harlston are just guards, making sure they don't escape. There are no benefits to being like them.

A while of thinking things like that, and then I ended up in a brief, dreamless slumber on my desk. I woke up light-headed and groggy, yet still scolding myself for doing such a thing. Attempting to make myself more alert, I stood up and shook myself, which made me slightly more awake, awake enough to check up on the patients at least.

I heard sobbing.

Coming from Martha's cell was the sound of crying, and I peered through the window to see her crouched over, covering her eyes with those hands of hers. In front of her was her mutt, lying dead, bloody, with flies swarming above it. I had a suspicion this would occur, yet I was still taken aback by the sight.

Lifting her head, she turned to see me, her eyes still wet. 'Hello.'

'Did you kill William?'

She turned away and continued her sobbing.

'Did you kill that dog?'

Still sobbing.

'Did you kill it or not?'

'It was the Lord who killed him,' said Martha, turning in my direction again, 'It was about Enfeld. Biting him made the Lord stronger, but...' Martha took a moment to calm down. 'The Lord said he wouldn't make a good follower. He said Enfeld had everything he hated about God.'

'This Lord of yours, knows about God?'

Martha pushed her face up to the window to speak to me. Tears still soaked her fur, and mucus dripped from her canine nose. 'He hates God, and is glad God's dead. When God ruled, everything was terrible, but he wants to make it right. And...' She began sobbing again. 'He sent me to help him, and I don't think I can.' Still crying, she leapt from the window and towards the carcass of her pet. 'I'm so sorry. I'm so sorry.'

Perhaps this is progress. She did kill the dog, but now she's realised the emotions death can bring. When she killed, she probably didn't think anything about those she killed, but now that a creature she loved had been killed, she probably could have a new perspective on it.

'Death is a terrible thing,' I said to her.

'I know.'

'Just think about all the people you killed. Don't you think they had friends and family who loved them? Those people are probably as miserable as you are about William.'

Martha whimpered. 'Please be quiet.'

I did as she told me to, and turned away, walking back to my quarters to complete some more work. Before I did though, I took one last look at Martha.

She crouched over her dog, and licked away its blood.

1st March 1887

We finally removed the dog cadaver from Martha's room today; such a thing was difficult considering her attachment to it. Removing that thing did nothing to lighten her spirits though, as she would continue to sit in her room for hours on end, staring at nothing. Occasionally, she would talk to us about the bright, green world her Lord was supposed to bring, but ended each telling with a moment of silence. Yesterday, I saw her looking through the window of her door, yet she didn't want to talk to me. In fact, it seemed like she was looking for something, or someone.

Enfeld still shows no signs of improvement ever since his transformation. Every day when I walk by his cell, I hear him pounding on the door, snarling. It is impossible to have a conversation with him, as he is usually pouncing about his room, looking for victims that don't exist. I try to ask him a question, but his only response was 'Let me out!'

What was Enfeld like in his human life? What did he tell me? Oh yes, I believe he was a cobbler, a job he found most tedious after a while. Before he became a werewolf, he looked for something new, and used to believe his transformation was God's cruel little joke. It wasn't God that did it to him though. I'd like to say it was the Devil, since so many people blame him for the world's ills. Many of those ills were caused by man, but this curse certainly wasn't, so maybe it was either God or the Devil or the Lord.

God works in mysterious ways, I am told. Maybe He had a purpose in creating this condition. He probably thought that too many people take humanity for granted, and to remedy this, He made them take on the form of beasts for a while. Then, when people learn the value of God's gift, He would take pity on them and release them from their curse.

Another theory: God is always testing us mortals, and this is another test. He gives this curse to a series of people just to see if they can resist it. Those who resist it are allowed to live normal lives, but those who don't will become animals and thus be hunted. Something of a variation on Noah's Ark, perhaps.

Theories that are completely unbelievable yet can be believed.

With the day spent on ponderings, theories and attempted conversations, night came quicker than I thought it would, and I found myself coming to Mr. Clentsworth, Mr. Landown, the few that remained. I told them to repress, I told them to remember what I had taught them, but before my eyes, they devolved into snarling beasts. Their words and groans became growls, accentuated with the sound of them pounding at the doors.

This place is only for containment.

I walked back to my quarters, and passed by Enfeld's cell. Despite the howling not too far away from him, he slept soundly. After I left him in peace, I found myself passing Martha's cell, which Harlston was just exiting from.

'Harlston?' I took him by surprise, just as he closed the door.

'Don't worry, she was fast asleep.'

'What were you doing?'

He pulled out a syringe. 'I think I have perfected the serum.'

'You have?'

'I have injected both Martha and Enfeld with it. It should work quickly, so by the morning, Enfeld should be back to his old self.'

'Will Martha become a regular werewolf?'

'Yes, I believe when the sun comes up, she will be briefly human, and then perhaps the both of you could go out. I believe the results will vary though. Enfeld has only briefly had the condition, while Martha has had it since birth, and I think, at the moment, that may mean it will only work for a short time on Martha. If so, I will tweak it to make it last longer.' Both of us stared at each other, saying nothing for a few seconds. 'I suppose I better use my remaining resources to see if I can find an actual cure now. Good night.'

And he left.

2nd March 1887

I had spent most of the night sitting outside Martha's cell, on a chair from the hall, just so I could be there if she does actually transform. Despite how quickly it took to arrive, the night was long. Even hearing the howls and grunts of those who succumbed did nothing to relieve the tedium. Somewhere around one o'clock, I did fall asleep, and slumbered soundly, as if to reclaim the hours of sleep I had lost from working. I only vaguely remember my dreams. I'm pretty sure I saw Martha's Lord, only I can't remember what he looked like, and I also remember seeing Harlston and Smertall.

I was awoken by a scream.

The shriek was so loud, I had an odd burst of energy upon waking, and the first thing I did after my sleep was peer into Martha's room. She was still screaming as the rays of sunshine coming through the window bathed her. Slowly, her fur shrunk away into her body, leaving only pale flesh behind. Her fangs flattened and her snout repressed into her face. As she screamed once more, I saw her pointed ears become rounder as they lowered. When all her fur had vanished, her tail was still squirming away. New hair sprouted from her head, snaking down to her shoulders, as her black, round nose elongated and thinned.

What struck me about the transformation was not how much she changed, but how little she had changed. I have seen many werewolves take on their human form again, but as Martha took on this new body, she seemed to keep the same shape as she did when she was a talking wolf, only somewhat taller.

The metamorphosis lasted for what seemed like hours, but it ended, and when it did, Martha collapsed to the floor. In a second, she forced herself to stand, wobbling as she did so, allowing me to get a better look at her human state, the form she should have been born with, free of the demon possessing her. While she looked around twenty years of age, her face had that look of childlike innocence. Her hair was a fair red in contrast to the matted grey fur she usually had.

She looked like my mother.

As I saw her observe her new body, I considered fleeing. Making her human, even temporarily, could kill the Lord in her mind, and this could send her into frenzy yet again. I didn't flee though. Instead, I watched as she raised her hands to her face, moving them about while wriggling the fingers. Then she began stroking her form with both of those hands, touching her face to feel her new nose.

Then she noticed me. 'I'm human,' was all she said. Her voice was different...softer.

I swallowed. 'Actually,' I told her, 'you are now....like all these patients here...you will be a wolf at night and human by day....at least...'

'Good,' she said, smiling. Her smile actually gave me relief this time. 'The Lord said this would happen. Now I can go out, and look at the other humans.' Her eyes widened. 'May I go out today?'

'I will consider it.' I left her for a minute so she could get used to her new humanity.

So now she was human. Not completely, of course, but she could probably still look unobtrusive in public. Should she go out in public though? I have taken some patients out into the world to help them when they feel alienated, and it has shown good results, so maybe this will help Martha. Would giving her this form make her less dangerous? She has lost her claws, her fangs, her malicious glare, would she not be meeker without them? She could still find a way to use violence though. She could still scratch someone, or bite them, and because she now looks more natural, those attacks would be more unexpected.

She did say the Lord wanted this to happen though. Perhaps it is also part of the Lord's will that she not kill while in this form? She could have killed only because she thought she had to, due to being a wolf. She knows humans shouldn't kill, because she wants those who do to go away, so could that mean she won't kill now?

I do want her to have a normal, human life, and I really do think I can give her one. I am aware I shouldn't rush things like this, but everything has passed so quickly recently.

As I sat, attempting to find answers, Harlston entered my quarters. As he entered, he laughed raucously, holding his stomach as he did so. 'What is so funny?'

His laughter ended in an instant, and he resumed his usual personality. 'It was Enfeld,' replied Harlston.

Oh yes. I had forgotten about him. 'Did the serum work on him?'

'It did, but he wasn't very pleased about it. Even now he's ranting and raving in his room, talking about how the world is mocking him again. It always gives me a chuckle when he talks about that.'

'Ah yes. Your serum worked on Martha too.'

'I know. She is quite beautiful.'

'I've been considering,' I told Harlston, finally turning in his direction, 'whether I should have Martha go out for a while now that she's taken that form.'

'If you do, you better do it soon. As I said, this new form may not last long. A few days and I believe she may be back to her unnatural form. Her brethren are such strange creatures. I almost regret changing Enfeld back; it would have been good to have more of her kind to study.'

'Enfeld is a human being, not an animal, and he should realise that.'

'Maybe he was born the wrong species. I mean, you do say the same about Martha.'

'Let us get back to her for a second.' I sat in my chair again. 'Now that she looks human, at least for a while, I have been thinking on whether or not we should take her out, or whether it would be too dangerous.'

'Certainly, we should. Today if possible. The more she learns about the human race, the better.'

'I don't think we should have her go out of the institution today, certainly we should give her some time to adjust.'

'She has been asking to go out quite a lot though. Certainly she would feel more comfortable with her new shape were her request fulfilled? Since her bite will have no effect at this moment, we could take her out without fear.'

'No, I think it would be better if I left it until tomorrow at the least. I need time to think about a step like this, and I'm not sure if she's ready.'

'I would think she's ready. She has been out in the city before, and then everybody feared her. Going out into the city when she will be inconspicuous should be simple enough for even someone like her.'

'No, I think it would be better for the both of us if I left it.'

'You may have a point. You can spend this time speaking to Enfeld, maybe get him to calm down.'

I looked at my desk, at all my notes about Enfeld, about Smertall, about Gramson and everyone. 'Very well. I shall try to calm him.'

'Good,' said Harlston, with a touch of joviality to his voice.

So, a little later, I made my way towards Enfeld's room, in hopes that he was in the mood to talk. As I did, I took a quick look at Martha, noticing her walking around the room. She had a strange way of walking while human; she held her arms in front of her as if trying to balance. I looked away and continued towards Enfeld.

When I came to his room, I found him sitting on his bed, head buried in his thick arms. He still grumbled.

'Hello!' I said, forcing a smile, 'Would you like to talk to me?'

Enfeld raised his head, revealing a smile of his own. 'Yes, I would like to talk. It's about what your friend did to me, isn't it?'

'Yes, it is. I know you're unhappy about it...'

'Of course I'm unhappy.' That smile vanished, making way for a fierce grimace. 'The best thing that ever happened to me and you get rid of it. Now I'm going to go back to those transformations that hurt and lose control every night. I thought you were trying to help me.'

'I am. I want you to suppress those transformations'

'Then you should have just left me the way I was. Give the needle to that wolf that goes on about the Lord, fine. But you should have left me as I am, then everything would have been fine.'

'You are a human being...'

'No, I'm not. I've been human for years and I hated every minute of it. When I took on that...always-wolf form, I started to realise how confused the world is.' That smile returned. 'If the world was fair,' he continued, laughing a little as he did so, 'I would be a beast, fighting for survival in the world, and that other wolf would be in some posh house, sipping tea and discussing politics.'

'Surely there are values to being human,' I asked him, 'Do we not have a richer culture? Are we not more civilised than the beast?'

'Don't give me anything about being civilised. No-one I've met can be called "civilised", so don't tell me how I should feel about humans.'

'Humanity is such a great gift, and you should not squander it.'

'A *gift?*' He laughed again. 'You're just pathetic. You're wasting your time talking to me. You aren't going to make me change my mind. Just get me back to being a wolf in control, let me out, and your life will be easier. I don't want your help anymore.'

'Well, if you don't want my help, then so be it.'

'Just go away.'

I did go away, just as he told me to. Maybe I should never talk to him again. If he wants to be an animal, I will let him live like one. This place can be for containment, but only for those who need it. People like him are what the world needs less of. I want a world without werewolves, and if those who enjoy being werewolves must be caged to achieve that goal, I suppose it must be done.

3rd March 1887

Just as one would expect, on the first night of being an actual werewolf, Martha succumbed to the nocturnal transformation. When she became a mindless wolf, I couldn't help but watch, seeing a body that could once hold conversations and share view degenerated into an animal. This morning, after she took on her human form, I found her giggling like a small child.

'Oh, thank you! Thank you!' she cried when she saw me peering at her, 'Last night, I felt so alive! I could hear the Lord congratulating me, saying this will help his time to come!' I said nothing. 'You said that you would take me out today. I could go into the city.' Those questions again. Should I? Shouldn't I? 'I would like to go out.' Her hand came from the window of her door, her slender human hand, lacking claws and fur, but still stained by faeces. 'I would like to know what being a human would be like. I may be the one that is helping the Lord change the world, but I would like to know what it feels like to be normal.'

I opened the door to her cell, and watched her stumble out, shaking, her hands still held out in front of her. Noting her way of walking, I took her by the hand to where I could prepare her for our outing.

First of all, due to the stains and smells of her 'material', she needed a bath before going out. I pulled out a wooden tub and filled it with water, and as I did so, Martha merely stood there, staring at everything I did with wide eyes. When the tub was full, and she placed her hand in the water, her eyes grew even wider. She took a small amount of the water in her palm, and poured it over her face, before rubbing the water into her skin. As if by instinct, she removed her gown, and slowly entered the tub. She placed her left foot in, allowing her toes to savour the liquid, then placed in her right foot, and then eased her body in, allowing the water to cover her completely. As she entered, she closed her eyes and gave a smile more feline than canine. Continually, she took water in her palm and poured it over her body, rubbing away the faeces and the filth, while I scrubbed her back.

After I helped her dry, I collected the clothing Harlston had offered me: a dark brown dress, complete with a corset and matching boots. When I showed them to Martha, she arched her eyebrows and said nothing. She continued to do nothing and say nothing as I fastened the corset around her waist, slipped the dress over her shoulders, placed her feet in the boots. After I had finished dressing, however, she sprung into some sort of dance, before saying, 'These feel strange.'

She did look like she belonged in the city, dawdling in the streets, eating at a pub, ignoring everyone else. If there was anything that seemed unusual, it would be her eyes, large saucers framed by grey bags.

'May I go out?' she asked, her face still beaming with juvenility.

My answer to her question was to take her by the hand, and escort her out of the institution. While she still wobbled as she moved, she looked more natural with me at her side. Though, when I opened the front door and felt the chilly breeze in my face, I stood as still as Martha did when I was dressing her. It was as if a hand was grabbing onto me, holding me back from allowing the wolf in a woman's body to walk the world.

'Move! Please, move!'Martha tugging on my arm and pleading set me walking in the direction of the city again. That hand holding me back had vanished once I was under her control. We walked quickly, because she walked quickly.

It took less time than I thought it would, but we managed to arrive into the main city, with its rickety buildings peering over us, the smoke reaching to pierce the sky, and the myriad people going about their business. The myriad victims.

I shouldn't have brought her out here. As I held her hand, I noticed it trembling. That fast pace she once had gone, and now she stepped through the streets carefully, looking around in every direction. There are no crimes being committed, so she shouldn't have the urge to kill, yet when I look at each of these people, the family with their recent purchases, the man with the stovepipe hat, I can't help but think of them being torn apart or turned into wolves.

Something caught Martha's attention, and she pulled me towards it. Unsurprisingly, it was a butcher's shop she had seen, and her eyes were fixed on the meat dangling on display. Her eyes were fixed on the display as if she were hypnotized for a matter of seconds, before she turned to me and said, 'The person who lives here must be a great hunter.'

She tried to release her arm from my grasp, but only ended up losing her balance and tumbling to the cobbled pavement. Giving a whinge, she attempted to make her way off the ground, until I was forced to take her by the hand and help her up myself. When she was back on her feet, she rubbed her face, wiping away the tears that dripped onto her cheeks.

'Do you feel alright?' I asked her, but she merely stood in silence. Only by pulling her arm a few times did she make any movement.

We found ourselves walking through the streets again, Martha still shaking slightly, and sometimes losing her footing. Her eyes still darted everywhere. Her movements earned us some puzzled looks from passer-bys, but I thought if I ignored it, she would ignore it.

Soon, we came to a marketplace, where one could hear the wooden structures of the stalls creaking in the breeze, rippling the striped roofs slightly. Another sight that aroused Martha's attention, one that made her drag me towards it.

'Hello!' said a chipper, chubby man behind a fruit stall. I rarely venture out into public these days, so to hear talk like that refreshed me after days of hearing grim accounts. 'How about an apple for your lovely daughter there?'

Ah, yes. An apple. It probably wouldn't hurt to have her try different foods. One can't live on slabs of meat. I gave the man a coin, and he tossed an apple into Martha's hand. She didn't eat it at first; instead, she observed it intently, as if it held an ancient secret. It was only when I gestured biting into the apple that she did so.

'I like this very much,' she said to the man, 'and I like that you called me lovely.'

'You're very welcome,' said the man, and after he said that, I pulled Martha away by the wrist before she could say anything more.

I was the leader for the remainder of the visit. With the monetary problems for our institution still being present, I didn't buy anything more, even if Martha took a special interest in it. Instead, I chose to take her to each stall and explain the purpose of its wares. When we approached a stall selling fish, I explained to Martha how humans fish and the benefits of eating them.

'I've seen fish,' she said, 'I don't eat them though. I think they are too beautiful to eat.'

I told her about farms, about craft, about how we are pushing ourselves forward when it comes to technology. I told her about humanity, and yet she didn't interact with it. Nobody talked to her, so she didn't talk to them.

She *can't* talk to them.

We perused the stores and their contents, with me explaining the purposes of each one, and then began to make our way into the main area of town. As we did, we saw a youngster, probably homeless by the look of his clothes, near us, his eyes fixed on Martha. Hearing him scuffle about, Martha turned in his direction, her eyes bulging.

A rotten peach hit her face.

That boy, that juvenile whelp began to laugh and ran away to safety. It would have been futile to try and follow him – I believe children are almost as alien as werewolves – but I found myself turning to Martha. She masked her face and its stains with her hands, those delicate human hands that would soon become claws. Her hands lowered slightly when I tried to comfort her, but in seconds, they covered her face again as she cried.

'I want to go home,' she said.

I shouldn't have brought her out here.

6th March 1887

I do not intend to take Martha out into the city in the near future, even if she looks more human. For the past two days since our outing, she has been mostly crying in a foetal position and screaming to the sky. And all because of one young boy and his play? At night though, she has succumbed to her primal wolf form, and has been eerily silent in that shape. When I called for her in that form, she slowly turned away from me. She hasn't howled, she hasn't gone into frenzy, she hasn't tasted that freedom.

She's in control of her nocturnal body.

While she has refused to talk to me during recent times, she has been calling for me today, her voice like a siren's chant.

I approached her cell and peered through the window, seeing her, still human, still wearing that gown, intently staring at her faecal matter as she tried to make more models out of it. 'Would you like to come in?' she asked, peering up from her work. Remembering what happened last time I entered, I merely stood still. 'I won't hurt you. I cannot now,' she added, burying her face in her hands again. Quickly, I entered and closed the door behind me, the smell of her waste being more familiar than rancid.

'I have noticed you have been very upset after that incident with the boy in the marketplace.'

'It made me think about humans. Because God is dead and the Lord is not powerful enough yet, they act in this bad manner because they have no-one to guide them. I'm afraid the Lord is going to die, and they will stay this bad forever.'

'Not everyone is like that,' I said, stroking her red hair, 'That man who gave you the apple wasn't bad, was he? I'm not bad, am I?'

'You are not,' Martha said, 'I know there are good humans because those are the people the Lord wants to keep. It is sad that there are good humans because those humans are weak and can do nothing against the bad ones. If the Lord makes them wolves, they will get rid of the bad humans, or the bad humans will be made their servants.'

'So you don't want to get rid of all the bad humans.'

'Some of them can be made good, that is what he said,' she said, staring at her sculptures, than to me, 'You don't want to be a wolf?'

'No, I don't.'

'Then when I change back, I won't bite you, because you are my friend. But you will want to become one. Then, I will bite you, because you will want me to.'

'Why will I want to become a wolf?'

'When am I changing back?'

'I don't know.'

'The Lord came to me last night. He said that my work as a human is done and I need to change back. If I do not, something may happen.'

'The Lord will die?'

'The Lord may not be powerful enough to take God's place, but he is still very powerful. He said that I should not spend a lot of time here anymore. He said that when I change back, you need to release me.'

I studdered away backwards, my hand reaching for the handle once again.

'He said he may come to this place and destroy it,' Martha continued, her eyes dominating her face. 'He said he may kill you and I do not want that to happen.'

'Martha,' I said firmly, 'There is no Lord.'

'What did you say?'

'There is no Lord,' I repeated, coming closer to her, 'He does not exist. He is merely a figment of your imagination.' Martha cowered as I told her this. 'You feel detached from humans because of your condition, Martha. You needed a friend, so you created the Lord in your mind because you were lonely.' I seized her by the shoulders and brought her face closer to mine. The bags under her wide eyes, the lines on her face, I saw them in more detail. 'There *isn't* a Lord, he will not kill anyone, and you have a companion in *me*.'

Martha shuddered. Nothing escaped from her mouth except slight wheezes.

'You could have handled that better.' Harlston peered at us through the door. When she noticed his presence, Martha ceased shuddering and smiled.

'Please, Harlston,' she said, 'Let me out. Change me back.'

'Harlston,' I said, turning around, 'Don't.'

'We might as well let her go free.' Harlston gave a small smirk. 'With our funding being cut and our monetary problems growing worse, we may be forced to anyway.'

I left the room, quickly closing and locking the door behind me before Martha could escape. Just before I exited, I saw her hobbling towards the door, and when it closed, she whinged. When I look at her, in her meek but spoiled human state, I see a wasted life, a wasted opportunity. I ponder on what could have been if she had been born a full human. If she had been free of the Lord's demands.

'It doesn't look good for the mortgage,' Harlston continued, 'So I am seriously wondering if we should let the patients go. All except Enfeld; we should just put him out of his misery.'

'You are not serious.'

'It doesn't really matter if they are no longer with us,' Harlston said, looking upwards, 'This place is really only to contain them anyway; they will find a new place to be contained within. Surely a cage can't be too expensive.'

'Harlston,' I replied through clenched teeth, 'I don't care about finance. All I want is for you to stay here and do your work.'

'Ah yes. The serum I gave Martha should be wearing off soon, I should make it last longer.'

'I want you to work on the cure. You have been working on that, haven't you?'

'Yes, I have. I think I still may need to study Martha's...natural form a little more though. And I do have a serum that will change her back, which, given how she feels as of now, would be a good idea to administer at this moment.'

'I want her to stay in this form for as long as possible, so she can get used to being human. I want her to let go of her wolf form. I want the Lord to die.'

I took Harlston through the corridors, letting him take a look at every patient we had. 'They all have had their lives ruined by a curse that we need to explain and eradicate. They are good people, inflicted with something they don't deserve. And you want me to stop taking care of them?'

'It's not that I want to, it is that we may have to. I've forgotten more than you'll ever know about these creatures, and I know what to do with them.'

'Look,' I held him by the shoulders so he could look me in the eyes. 'If we are low on money, we should do whatever good we can with it. You are to spend whatever time you have trying to destroy that infliction once and for all. You are not to leave this institution for any purpose.'

Harlston turned around and walked towards his quarters. 'Very well.'

10th March 1887

Remembering how I had spoken to her yesterday, the first thing I made sure to do today was to visit Martha. As I approached her cell, I stumbled about as I did so, having obtained less sleep than usual. Not because of a high amount of howling and gnashing, but rather due to the silence.

When I walked up to Martha's cell, I saw that she had reverted back to her anthropomorphic form. A wolf with appendages stretched out, and with a warped body, still wearing that stained gown. Peering through the door window, I saw her looking at her hands, her claws. She smiled, but her face did not bear the hideous Cheshire Cat grin she had in her more jovial moods.

Her claws were bared. One was close to her neck.

'Martha?'

Upon hearing the sound of my voice, she cowered to the back of the room, making that gibbering sound from yesterday.

'I understand you may be frightened, but, I'm always here if there is something you wish to talk about.'

Continuing to cower, she clawed at the air in front of her, like a cat trying to frighten away some creature. I should have taken this as a sign to leave her alone, but I stayed firm, knowing that I couldn't let anything happen to her. Thus, I slowly opened the door to her cell, letting the aroma off her artwork flood my nostrils. She screamed. A scream that sounded like nothing from human or beast.

'Martha?'

'Lord?' she whispered, looking away from me.

'Is there anything you wish to discuss?'

Finally, she turned in my direction. 'Why are you here? I'm not human anymore.'

'I know,' I said to her as I closed the door. 'Isn't that what the Lord wanted?'

'You...you said that he was not real.'

Despite the miserable tone she used for that sentence, that little spark of hope ignited once again. 'You don't believe in him anymore?'

'I was talking to him...when I changed back. He heard you when you said he wasn't real. He needs belief. It makes him stronger.'

At this point, I knew my fingers should have been wrapping around the door handle, but I remained still, as did Martha.

'He wants me to kill you.'

I sighed as I turned to face her. 'Do you want to kill me?'

Her eyes did not blink. 'No,' she replied, matter-of-factly. Freezing in place, her eyes still fixed themselves on me. She had become a statue, even in a pose like the lions that frame certain buildings.

'Did you like being human?' I asked her, unsure of the exact reason why.

'It...it wasn't what I thought it would be like. It was...dizzy.'

Knowing full well what her Lord wanted to do with me, I came closer to her, and stroked her fur again, feeling those scars. This made her spring to life, but only for a minute, as she grabbed a hold of me.

Her claws were no longer bared.

I held her close, continuing to run my fingers through her thick fur. As she pressed her body against me, I was reminded that I still had my gun in my pocket. If she knew I had it, and what it was, what would her reaction be?

Soon, she let go, resuming that lion pose with the mechanical stare. When another 'Lord?' escaped her lips, I walked away from her and left the cell, carefully letting the door squeak shut. Taking one last look before moving on to other business, I saw that she remained in that pose, which gave me an uneasy sense of comfort.

With her still on my brain, I made my way to visit Clentsworth. I haven't spoken to that man in a while, and he probably has accumulated more demons in my absence. Of course, when I saw him, he was whispering unintelligible things to himself, what someone in my trade has encountered time and time again. That whispering ceased when he saw me arrive, and was replaced by a low laugh.

'May I speak to you?'

'No.'

'Why not?'

'I can't talk. I need to get out.'

I have feared that this institution was made only to contain those who wanted to be contained. Now, with requests like these, should that fear be through with? Or is it another fear altogether?

'I've...I've got to go. I've got to move...'

'Would you like a spell in the gardens?'

'No, that's not good enough...the outside has been calling me, I keep hearing something telling me to leave this place...'

'I remember when you first came here,' I said, hands in my pockets, 'you said that you were physically unable to go outside. Every time you tried, you would freeze in place.'

'It's not like that anymore...please, just open this door.'

I should be able to help him. I should be able to tell him why he shouldn't. I should have calmed him down. All I did was just stand there, contemplating if having him leave this plane would be fulfilling his request.

12th March 1887

I opened this institution to help me, and my patients, finally fully understand lycanthropy. To control it, to find its causes, and to destroy it. I have given Harlston experiments and assignments to do, but he tends to keep things from me. While he may have uncovered some rather interesting things in his time, I have still considered replacing him. Still, who else would be willing to work with, of all things, werewolves?

My willingness to understand this condition was the reason Martha was brought into our vicinity. She was another wrinkle in this puzzle, and thus she had to be examined as closely as possible. Her form, her make-up, her 'Lord'. I have spoken to her several times, yet I still cannot truly comprehend her, her brain, or her form, or if she can, or should, be cured.

I have pondered if there are things in life that are not meant to be comprehended. Like God, ironically enough. If, as I have suspected, the werewolf is meant to be part of God's great plan, then perhaps I am working against God, or the Lord.

No, the Lord is a delusion. Something I have had to hammer into Martha's head. Perhaps I may have to do it for everyone else here.

Today I received another letter from Mrs. Smertall: *I appreciate all you have done for my dear Harold, but I have become very worried about him recently. Not because he is succumbing again, he is doing very well with that, but it is during the day with which I am most concerned. He has been entering into violent moods- yesterday I saw him tossing about things in our kitchen – and afterwards, he would break into sobs. Yet he has been fairly calm at night, and does not transform at all. I am disturbed by his behaviour, but I do not wish for him to return to your institution...*

She shouldn't have come here.

It's because of her Clentsworth wants to leave. It's because of her Enfeld loathes me all the more. It is even likely that she brought about some of my patients' conditions. She is not human or animal; rather she is the embodiment of lycanthropy, its ugliness given flesh and bone.

She is mocking me.

I realize that such a statement may be an overused one, considering both Smertall and Enfeld have said it about her, but it is still an apt phrase to use. When I first saw her, I saw a fascinating beast that could have solved all our problems, a sad soul led astray by her own deformities. Now when I think of her, all I can see is her grin.

She is a monster. Monsters must be destroyed.

I still keep my gun on me most of the time. My father's gun.

I did not tell Martha everything about my mother. I did not tell her about how I woke up one morning to see mother cling onto the shoulders of my father, sobbing and wailing. Most of her words were unintelligible, but I know she said, 'Kill me' several times. As a child, I understood death well, and had spent hours pondering what death would be like, but I did not understand why someone would want to die. I did not watch what followed, but I still heard it.

My father told me it had to be done. He comforted me after it had transpired. I did understand why it had to be done, and that's why I opened this institution.

Have people asked me to kill them? Yes, but that is a sign they should live, as they actually acknowledge they should repress. More than can be said for Enfeld and Martha. I don't see Martha as a person actually; she seems to be an idea brought into reality. I wished that something like her existed, so I believed she did so hard she became real. I did not foresee the influence she would have, and, as my responsibility, I have to remedy that.

How fitting that it should be Martha that would interrupt my train of thought, with a fierce delivery of caterwauling and growling. The noises I heard from her were not the tormented cries of the insane, but merely a childish temper tantrum. One aspect to this position I acknowledged long ago is that it can often feel like parenting, but hearing Martha's tantrum, I almost laughed. A great Messiah, acting like this?

Still, if she was upset, it was my duty to go and care for her. I promised her I would, so I left my office and walked down the halls towards her cell. Despite the chill present in the corridors, I still felt beads of sweat drip down my back. When I finally reached her door,she had ceased her noise. Despite that, I entered her cell, without her even asking me to.

'You,' she said when she heard me enter, 'I was just talking about you.'

'Were you?'

'It was...the Lord. He still wants to kill you...' She hung her head, while the rest of her body froze into that statue pose again.

'You shouldn't do what he says.'

She lifted her head to look at me, before letting it down again.

'Martha,' I said, coming closer to her. 'Harlston and I are still working hard on perfecting that serum.' Her head lifted up again. 'Just think, you won't have to listen to the Lord. You'll be human; you'll have a normal life.' Her response to this was another low growl, and turning her head towards the wall.

She can't stay like this. She can't be human.

I reach into my pocket.

What else can I do?

'Martha?' She turned to me and saw the gun in my hand. It was only as she looked at me that I remembered she had past experience with hunters.

Her eyes don't blink. She sat still.

A slight smile.

One pull.

One pull was all it took. Losing control of my body for a moment, I aimed the gun at her breast, and pulled the trigger.

One pull was all it took for her. A legendary creature terrorising England and this was all I had to do. Her body lay among the faecal matter and urine and uneaten bits of meat. Her eyes and mouth lay wide open.

When I first discovered her, I had become fixated on her form, having see nothing like it before, but had grown used to it over time. Now, once again, I feel that fixation, as I stand in a puddle, telling myself that this bizarre carcass was once alive. A feeling I have encountered while observing the mummies at the museum, but this was a lively creature that had its life taken by me, or whatever made me use that gun.

Forcing myself to leave, I opened the door to be greeted by Harlston, an expression on his face more terrifying than Martha's grin.

15th March 1887

I have spent many long months working with these creatures. I have tried to provide for them, I have persuaded them to suppress their transformations, I have spoken with them about matters I have pondered on for years. Now I find myself wanting nothing more to do with them.

For the past few days, I have spent my time in my quarters, looking over all the notes I have collected, in hopes of finding something that could be of any use. I rarely leave my room, except to try and stop my patients from succumbing. I have done that less recently though. Imagine, after what I've done, telling them not to lose control of themselves and murder.

Today, as has become the practice for me, I stayed in my quarters, studying every note, getting as much sleep as I could. I find my dreams becoming much more vivid, featuring the cold eyes of Harlston, Martha as both a human and the hybrid, Gramson and Smertall demanding me to come back to them, and mother.

I always see mother. I can see her when I walk down the halls, when I look out of the window, when I look at Martha, still lying there in her cell. I see her, and she sees me. Whenever I look at Martha's body among her sculptures, her face bears the most hideous snarl. I still hear Martha's voice, and I can still see her walking in the halls. Maybe the reason I find myself here is because I see her less here. That judgmental face always distracts from my work. Still, I requested that we keep her corpse inside that cell. It was not to be moved, not even for experimental purposes.

As I lay, observing my notes, Harlston entered. The entrance took me aback, making me fall over backwards in my chair. Hearing a laugh from Harlston twisted my stomach.

'Hello,' he said, 'Would you like some tea?'

I watched as he placed a cup on my desk. 'Martha...' I said, beginning to stand up, 'You saw me...'

'Don't worry about it,' said Harlston, sipping his own cup, 'She was going to die anyway. And you likely had good intentions while doing so. You always do.'

Staring at my cup, I did not drink. 'I just...'

'You can't believe you did that. They never do.'

I held up my cup. Tea entered my throat, yet did nothing to soothe me. 'I thought I was putting her out of her misery...I think no matter what we did for her, she would always talk about the Lord...'

Putting down his cup, Harlston placed a finger on his chin. 'I have been thinking about what Martha has told us, and I like to think her Lord is real.'

Hearing this, I collapsed onto my desk.

'Figuratively speaking. He seems to represent something significant. A figure that exposes people, that strives to recreate the world into something more...fitting. I have felt a force like that during my escapades, even before Martha arrived here. As much lunatics as I see proclaiming themselves God, believing in a higher force that is making you do something for him, is a fine way to keep your sanity.' He lifted up the cup again, and guzzled the last drops down. 'You strived to make her believe the Lord was not real, and look what has happened to you.'

Losing my energy, I still replied. 'I really thought I could cure her...'

'You could if you had tried harder. Or perhaps if you had put more faith in me.'

There followed a moment of silence between us, before Harlston departed, and I fell asleep.

This night, after the heavy slumber over my array of notes, I noticed the sun beginning to set, so I stumbled over to my door, expecting to hear the cries and snarls, but instead being greeted to silence.

The doors were open.

Martha was gone.

The entrance fully open, I was greeted to every one of her sculptures, her artwork, yet no sign of the late creator. There is no human, no wolf, no mixture of the two, only the small figures in a circle, laughing at me.

Harlston.

I ran down the corridors, my feet echoing all the while, noticing how many other cells were let empty. The stench of blood, urine and faeces drifted through, a powerful spirit revelling in the escapes.

Harlston did this. He disobeyed orders. After all we've been through, after all we've tried to treat these souls...

A letter lay by Harlston's door. Scraps of paper sitting there, waiting to be read. I picked them up and took them to my office.

This is what it read:

I apologize for not following your orders, but I can no more keep up the masquerade. When I responded to your calls for aid on your mission, I did intend to study werewolves, but not because I wanted to cure them. That thought may have found itself worming into my brain a few times, but it was because of how interesting the creatures are.

I have worked at many institutions, have studied and taught at many universities and have been on many expeditions with cohorts and fellow scientists. I am, as they say, a jack of all trades, but I would not say I was a master of none. I have done several things, and if there is one thing I have picked up from all these ventures, it is a total detest for humanity.

Have you not been in the typical university? Have you not observed the ignorant children that attend there, those that have no intention of learning or becoming a success? And there are those scientists, who may have their books and stats, and carry around that grotesquely arrogant attitude because of it.

Every person I have met, every student I have lectured to, every friend I have shared a drink with, they were all monsters. All of them wanted to be loved, all of them wanted fame and fortune, but none of them deserved it. There was something inside them, a tiny little urge that belied their joyful exterior. Some may call it their 'souls'.

What you do not understand about the werewolf is that it is a way of letting that darkness free; it is when people show you who they really are. Werewolves make no pretensions about themselves, they show you who they really are. Only when one becomes a werewolf does one seek help about their personality, only then will they actually ask to be improved. To be human.

They think to be human is to be clean and sinless, when it is quite the opposite. Werewolves are probably the most human of us all. Yet the people we have had here refuse to accept that. Even Enfeld, who craved that form, wanted it because he wanted to be an animal.

The very day I began studying werewolves I tried to recreate the curse. I would find those I thought kept their true desires, their true selves most hidden and give them the curse. It would be a test; my idea was that they would finally show how they really were by not suppressing, by welcoming the freedom their new forms give them.

The likes of Smertall and Gramson may have repressed, and I commend them for it; they are the type of people the Lord wants to keep. Oh yes, the Lord.

Martha's coming was a blessing; when she came, I fully realised why I studied her brethren. I always thought the werewolf was a message from a higher force, and she pinpointed that force, and every night would tell me of the world I wanted. One without pretensions, where everyone knew who they truly were, where the types of humans I hated most would either die or be the lowest animal.

She needed me though. I had to show the poor child what she needed to know. She needed to see how ugly the human race truly was, so I made her like them so she could get the closest look possible. She needed people beside her, so I tried to find a way to make the common werewolf like her.

Yes, that is what the Lord didn't tell her. While her bite may have made normal people werewolves, it was quite useless on those already cursed with nightly transformations. I injected Enfeld with another serum to give him that form. I thought that because he hated humanity like I did, he would be a fine addition to the Lord's followers. He was an idiot, though, and thought following the Lord only mean devolution. I feel ashamed about that mutt.

And you killed her.

Poor Martha still had so much to learn and you murdered her before she could reach her potential. You probably thought the Lord would die as well if you did that. Maybe the other werewolves would be cured if the Lord were to fall. I can still feel the Lord's presence though, and Martha still lives on in spirit. I have taken her corpse to remind my followers of what they will be fighting for.

Have you not learned from her? Have you not learned from me? That 'exorcism' I performed proves God no longer has any power, and how Martha acted when taking on a form like ours proves what I've always thought of our brethren, as did your murder.

Together, me and the werewolves and Martha will create the perfect world. One without lies, where every murder is necessary, and everyone will get what they deserve. It will be a beautiful world, where its beauty will lie in its ugliness. Everything happens for a reason, and the Lord is the reason I worked with you for so many years.

Don't try and find us, because the Lord will find you.

Signed,
Jack Harlston

THE END?